I0534914

GRANNY ON BOARD

A SECRET AGENT GRANNY MYSTERY BOOK 7

HARPER LIN

This is a work of fiction. Names, characters, organizations, places, events, and incidents are either products of the author's imagination or are used fictitiously.

GRANNY ON BOARD

Copyright © 2019 by Harper Lin.

All rights reserved.

No part of this book may be reproduced, or stored in a retrieval system, or transmitted in any form or by any means, electronic, mechanical, photocopying, recording, or otherwise, without express written permission of the author.

ISBN: 978-1-987859-69-0

www.harperlin.com

ONE

My boyfriend, Octavian, had really outdone himself this time.

As if figuring out a way to alert the police when we were kidnapped inside a miniature submarine or helping me with a murder investigation at the Cheerville Country Club wasn't enough, now he had gone one better.

He was treating me to a cruise.

The cruise was a gift for my seventy-first birthday. Octavian had shown some sleuthing skills to find that out. It wasn't the sort of information I shared. The sneaky fellow had asked my grandson, Martin, when we were all having milkshakes at Fatburger one day. He must have asked when I had gone to get extra napkins to clean up Martin's inevitable spill. Martin, being thirteen, of course didn't know my birthday, so Martin asked my son, Frederick, who probably had to look it up. Then the information got passed down the line back to Octavian, and my boyfriend popped the question.

No, not *that* question, but whether I'd like to go on a cruise with him.

I'm Barbara Gold. Age: barely seventy-one. Height: five foot five. Eyes: blue. Hair: gray. Weight: none of your business. Specialties: undercover surveillance, small arms, chemical weapons, Middle Eastern and Latin American politics. Current status: retired CIA agent, widow, and grandmother to a teenager who seemed to be in cahoots with my boyfriend.

Addendum to current status: wondering just how serious this relationship was getting.

Addendum to addendum: feeling a mixture of joy, terror, and a complete bafflement as to whether I was ready for this or not.

I must admit that my first reaction was to say no. I'm fond of the old dear, but a cruise? It would involve a flight down to Florida together, then getting on a ship, staying in separate cabins (he had been most clear on that), and sailing around the Caribbean for ten days.

One thing I learned in all the international operations I did, was that you didn't really know someone until you traveled with them. I'd known agents who were capable back at base, lots of fun on R&R, and who turned out to be grade A pains in the you-know-what when in the field. There's something about being in forced proximity with another person that reveals all their flaws and annoying personality traits.

And your own too.

Until now, Octavian and I had spent no more than a whole day together, with the knowledge that at the end of it, we would go back to our separate houses and separate lives. Being on the same ship for ten whole days could scupper our blossoming relationship.

Or—and I have to admit I feared this just as much—take it to another level.

And there was another problem—it was a seniors' cruise.

"A seniors' cruise?" I said when he told me. We were sitting at the Ticktock Cafe, the noisiest place in town because of the hundred or so ticking clocks on the walls. I raised my voice as much to be heard as to express my surprise.

"What's wrong with a seniors' cruise?" Octavian asked.

"Well ... it will be a bunch of ... seniors. Won't it be boring?"

"Not at all. I've been on them before, and I've been on regular cruises. The problem with regular cruises is you get too many younger people. The dance floor is packed, and the music is terrible. And then everyone is stumbling past your cabin drunk at three in the morning causing all kinds of commotion. The seniors' cruises are much more civilized, and they aren't boring. They have lots of activities."

I studied the brochure from the cruise company. It did look like a nice ship, with a pool, several Jacuzzis, a disco, a casino (I'd pass on that), four restaurants, three cafes, three bars, a drama theater, and a movie theater. It also stopped at a couple of Caribbean islands with arrangements for day trips on shore.

I considered my options. It was this or have a quiet birthday at home with my family. Much as I love my family, they do not throw good birthday parties. A mediocre supermarket cake, a couple of presents I didn't really need, and a birthday card that I was morally required to keep on my mantelpiece until the next birthday rolled around.

Or I could throw the dice and see what would happen with Octavian.

Having been a CIA operative for all my professional career, one could say I was a risk-taker. So I decided to take the risk. What was the worst that could happen?

Famous last words.

TWO

The *Silver Siren* was Surf n' Sun Cruise Line's dedicated seniors' cruise ship. It was a huge thing, moored at the pier in Fort Lauderdale. I had never been on a cruise or even seen a cruise ship up close. It looked like a city block of high-rise apartment buildings. I marveled that the thing could float.

The white deck and superstructure gleamed in the Florida sun. On the prow was painted the profile of an older man and woman looking out to sea, with rugged features and silver hair like a pair of retired Greek deities. Rows of portholes showed the locations of the cabins, with larger windows for those on the upper deck. The suites even had porches. You could sit out on deck chairs watching the sea.

Octavian and I stood in line with a few hundred

other senior citizens filing through the welcome center before going up the gangway. The amount of gray hair, canes, walkers, and unfocused grumpiness in the line was depressing. I was getting a bad feeling about this.

While it was only natural that most of my friends were my age, I had made a point in my retirement to spend a large amount of time with younger people. I had moved to Cheerville to be with my son, daughter-in-law, and grandson after all. I had even taken my grandson and his friends out for pizza. Ever taken a group of thirteen-year-olds out for pizza? I've been in battles quieter than that.

So I wasn't too keen on spending the next ten days with only old people. Being around old people for long periods of time made me feel ... fossilized.

"Ready for some fun?" Octavian asked, giving me one of those winning smiles of his. No one on the far side of seventy has any right to such a good pair of teeth. They were even real.

"Sure," I said, keeping up a brave face.

We got to the counter, where a pair of young women with pasted-on smiles checked our tickets and handed us information brochures and the keys to our cabins. I noticed the brochures were all in large print. They hadn't even asked if we needed that.

Then they took our luggage, which would go on board separately and be delivered to our cabins. "That's *Silver Siren* service for you!" one of the young women chirped.

They indicated the gangway, which wasn't one of those sloping little boards like you see in movies. A large door big enough to drive a truck through had actually opened up in the side of the ship, and a platform the width of a two-lane highway allowed all the passengers to board. A good thing, too, because a lot of those passengers couldn't have handled an incline. They could barely handle a completely level two-lane highway. I hadn't seen that many walkers, canes, and mobility scooters since I stopped going to the Cheerville Senior Center.

One of those mobility scooters had stopped scooting and was stuck sideways, blocking part of the path. Somehow a few wheelchairs, walkers, and more mobility scooters had gotten tangled and caused a backlog of passengers who were trying to help untangle the whole mess but really only causing more of a traffic jam.

We got stuck in back, trying to peek over a sea of gray and bald heads to see if a group of frantic sailors was having any luck fixing the whole mess.

After a few minutes, it became apparent that

they were not. People began to grumble. People began to tut-tut. People began to say, "Back in my day ..."

Now I don't want to sound like a grumpy old person who complains about every little thing, but if there is one thing I cannot stand, it's grumpy old people who complain about every little thing. Life's hard enough without being surrounded by crabby people, and these sailors had a tough enough job without getting grumped at by a few hundred senior citizens who were supposed to be here enjoying themselves.

The grumbling was rising in pitch. Canes were shaken in the air. Shouts of "I'll complain to the management!" mingled with "Wait until I tell my travel agent. He'll never do business with you again!"

It was time to take action.

"Excuse me," I said, trying to edge my way through the press. I barely got a step forward.

I tried a different tactic.

"I need the restroom, and I forgot my adult undergarments!" I shouted in a loud, clear voice.

The crowd parted like the Red Sea. Or the Gray Sea, I should say.

I strode to the mobility scooter. A sailor had the panel off and was inspecting the electric motor. The woman riding it sat impassively, not even looking at the sailor fiddling with the engine, waiting for someone else to fix her problems for her.

While I am not a trained mechanic or engineer by any stretch of the imagination, in the field, I had to know a little bit about everything and to be able to solve problems quickly. I peered over the shoulder of the sailor who was on his knees trying to figure out how to get the mobility scooter started. Some of the other sailors were talking about carrying her in, but the combined weight of the scooter and its passive occupant looked prohibitive. The rising anger of the crowd demanded an answer, and quickly.

One of the sailors was on a walkie-talkie. From the half of the conversation I could hear, he was calling the ship's engineer. It sounded like the engineer was below decks and wouldn't make it for several minutes, though.

A few minutes too late.

"Let us through!" rose from hundreds of warbling throats.

The grumbling, hobbling crowd began to push forward. A woman shrieked as a wheelchair tipped and nearly overturned. A couple of people near the front got shoved and would have fallen, but the press of the crowd kept them upright. Someone was going to faint pretty soon if this kept up.

"Please keep calm!" one of the sailors shouted in anything but a calm voice. "We'll have this solved in a minute."

He and his shipmates pushed back.

"Unhand me!" some irate senior citizen said, rapping a sailor on the skull with his cane.

This was turning ugly quickly. I stopped looking at the scene around me. The best way out of this was to focus on the engine.

Then I saw the problem. The circuit between two connections had broken. The metal strip on the circuit board had taken a knock somehow, and part of the metal had chipped off. The wires were still in place—the sailor had been looking for something obvious like a loose wire, and that's why he couldn't find the problem—but it didn't matter, because the circuit board itself was faulty.

I reached between the burly shoulders of the line of sailors trying to gently but firmly push back the angry mob and plucked a hairpin off the nearest gray bun.

"Stop! Thief!" the woman shouted.

Then she tried to punch me. Actually tried to punch me.

Luckily her aim was off, and she missed, instead landing her fist on the square jaw of the nearest sailor.

"Ow!" she wailed. "You've broken my hand. I'm going to sue!"

I went back to the mobility scooter and clipped the hairpin between the two connections, and the engine hummed to life.

"Get going!" I shouted to the woman on the mobility scooter over the roar of the crowd.

"It's about time," she said, turning her scooter to face front and zipping into the ship.

"You're welcome!" I called after her.

The sailors moved back slowly, allowing a few people at a time through the cordon while some of their shipmates untangled the mess of walkers and wheelchairs. Soon the crowd was moving forward again in a frowning, grumbling mass. At least it was a frowning, grumbling, orderly mass.

Octavian reached me where I was standing to one side next to a cluster of sailors.

"You all right?" he asked, taking my hand.

"Did I mention I don't like being around large numbers of people my age?"

"Once or twice," he said, abashed. "Or perhaps more."

Immediately I felt sorry. He was trying to give me a nice vacation, and here I was grumbling like the herd that had just stampeded its way onto the ship. The fact that I had good cause didn't change anything.

I gave him a peck on the cheek. "Never mind. It will get better from here on."

We entered the ship together, coming into a giant ballroom. A huge crystal chandelier hung from the ceiling. To one side stood a large round stage around which curved a sweeping staircase going up to the next deck. Signs pointed every which way, giving directions to the rooms. The crowd broke into smaller streams, heading off down hallways or up the stairs. Some lingered by the stage, where a band was playing.

And what an odd band. A lead singer who looked to be in his eighties but with muscles to shame any gym jock a third his age was singing a tune while wearing only running shorts, sneakers, and a muscle T-shirt. His band was made up of four women not much younger than he was who were similarly outfitted. They all looked in remarkable health, too, although I noticed a walker tucked behind the drummer's chair and a cane leaning against the stool on which the lead guitarist sat.

The song sounded familiar too.

"I'll spot you, baby,

I don't mean maybe

When you do your bench presses

I'll stroke your long tresses."

"It's—" I began.

"Tony Iron and the Bar Belles," Octavian finished.

We gaped at a legend from our youth.

Tony Iron had been the heartthrob of our generation. Just as Octavian and I hit puberty, Tony Iron had hit the charts with songs like "Power Lifting Love" and "When I do Squats, I Call the Shots." America was on a fitness craze that decade, and he sang the songs that everyone sweated to.

Being teenyboppers at the time, we weren't going to the gym, but the girls loved Tony Iron because he was so handsome and muscular, and the boys loved him because he was always surrounded by the gorgeous (and amazingly toned) Bar Belles. These people actually did workout routines on stage while going through their songs.

I hadn't heard them in decades. They're one of those bands from your youth where you occasionally find yourself humming a tune of one of their songs, but you never get around to looking up whatever happened to them.

What happened, it turned out, was that they had grown old and were giving concerts on seniors' cruises.

Seeing them like this was like mortality giving me a slap in the face. I had an enduring image of Tony Iron and the Bar Belles from my younger years —Tony looking like a Greek statue with a tan and a pompadour, the Bar Belles gorgeous and strong. They had been the paragons of youth and beauty. In fact, the Bar Belles had been my first female role models of women who were tough and yet remained feminine. They could bench-press their own weight, and their mascara wouldn't run. The whole band used to run marathons for various charities and look just as good at the end as they did at the beginning.

They weren't running any marathons now. They moaned through one of their old numbers, "Kissing Between Reps," at a slower tempo than I remembered it. Tony tried to strut and flex like he did before, but he looked tired, a shadow of his former self. His pompadour was still shiny black without a touch of gray, and this obvious dye job only made him look older. The Bar Belles stumbled through their notes, barely looking at the audience.

The whole scene made me depressed.

I glanced at Octavian. He looked anything but depressed.

His eyes shone, his mouth open in a big grin, and he was softly singing along to himself.

"Were you a fan?" I asked.

"Weren't we all?"

I chuckled. "I suppose so."

"Tony Iron was a hero of mine. I was a ninety-pound weakling in middle school. Then I sent away for his Tony Iron Muscles of Steel Training System."

"The one advertised in the comic books?"

"That's right. It worked! I ended up on the football team. I even played in college."

"I didn't know that."

"Oh, my athletic days are well behind me. Now I'm what they refer to as spry."

I smiled. And here I thought Octavian only did seniors' yoga to pick up women.

We watched until Tony Iron and the Bar Belles finished their set. We cheered, stayed for an encore of "Doing Curls for the Girls," and cheered again as they hobbled offstage.

Well, only two of the Bar Belles hobbled. The other two more or less walked, and Tony Iron strutted, actually strutted. I thought people weren't allowed to strut after they were eligible for a senior citizen's discount.

After that we headed upstairs to our deck, marveling at being inside a ship that looked for all the world like a five-star hotel. We made it to our cabins, which were right next to each other. Octavian stopped and turned to me.

"Let's get settled in, and then we'll meet in half an hour. We can go on deck to watch the ship leave port."

"All right."

He gave me a peck on the cheek.

"Oh, look at the lovebirds! Already getting romantic, and we haven't even left port yet."

I turned to see a woman in her sixties in front of a gaggle of similarly aged women. They all wore bright sundresses and looked like a moving flowerbed. All had dye jobs to rival Tony Iron's. The woman who had spoken, who sported hair that was blond beyond her years, smiled and extended her hand.

"Hello, I'm Georgina."

And that was how we met Georgina Branch. That was when the whole trip got complicated.

THREE

Georgina Branch gave us a warm smile and said, "We're all in the same hall here. These are my friends," she said, motioning vaguely behind her. "We all took cabins in the same hall so we could make sure we're all having fun. We were wondering who got the other two cabins on B Deck, Hall 5, and now we know!"

We introduced ourselves. As the other women—there were five of them—started to introduce themselves, Georgina cut in.

"We're all just getting settled in, and we were planning on meeting back here in twenty minutes so we can go up on deck and get the best spot for seeing the ship leave port. Want to come?"

Octavian and I looked at each other and shrugged. That was very close to our plan.

"We'd be honored, ladies," Octavian said, making a slight bow.

Georgina smiled. Her gaggle of friends giggled. A bow may have been old-fashioned even when we were kids, but there's something about it that gets into a woman's heart.

We all split up and went to our respective cabins. I have to say, I was impressed. Other than a porthole for a window and a slight curve in the outer wall, it looked just like a regular, if undersized, hotel room. Besides a comfy bed (complete with a chocolate on the pillow, an essential ingredient to any good hotel stay), there was a small table and two chairs, a decent-sized closet, and a small bathroom with a shower but no tub. There was also a big-screen TV that looked ungainly on the small stretch of wall allowed for it. The thing would probably hurt my eyes if I turned it on. It didn't matter, I hardly watched television at home, let alone when I was on vacation.

I unpacked, freshened up, and took a peek out my porthole. It gave a good view of our pier and a freighter unloading shipping containers at the next pier over. The porthole was too small for me to fit through, and there was no second porthole in the bathroom. Yes, an odd thought, but my CIA training had made looking for a back exit an automatic reaction. This cabin was a dead end. That unsettled me somewhat.

Coming back into the hallway, I found Georgina Branch and her coterie already there. They had made an admiring circle around Octavian, who was flashing them his winning smile.

"Ah! There she is," Georgina said. "You need to be on time if you want to keep up with the fun! Let's go on deck."

I slipped through the crowd of Octavian's admirers and was rewarded with Octavian's hand around my waist. He usually didn't do that; he was obviously sending a signal to our new friends.

Fine by me.

Georgina was right. Going up on deck a bit early did get us a good spot. We beat the crowd and ended up right on the prow. Well, almost on the prow. The very tip of the prow was chained off with a notice, "Imitating scenes from *Titanic* is not allowed, as it poses a safety risk."

They could have added that recalling a film where a luxury liner sinks and hundreds of people drown is probably not the best way to keep spirits up during a cruise.

Nevertheless, we had a great spot. The sun was shining, and we looked out across a sweeping view of the harbor. Freighters and luxury yachts gleamed in the sunlight. Another cruise ship was just pulling out, slowly moving past the last of the piers and into the open sea.

The deck began to fill up, and Georgina's friends, whose names I still hadn't learned, praised her for her foresight. I got the impression that they spent a lot of time praising her.

After a few minutes, the ship's horn blew a long, low blast that reverberated in our chests. I glanced around to see if anyone had keeled over from having their pacemakers stopped, but apparently the engineers who designed pacemakers had foreseen that senior citizens like going on cruises and made their product immune to ships' horns.

Slowly we began to pull out. Everyone cheered. I found myself cheering alongside them. I'm not really the cheering type. The only time I've spontaneously cheered was when our military transport plane left Kabul airport many years before.

If you ever took off successfully from Kabul airport, you'd cheer too.

Kabul is surrounded by mountains, and while we held the city, the Taliban held the mountains. So anytime a plane took off from the airport, it would attract several Stinger antiaircraft missiles. These are heat-seeking missiles, so the plane would take off, ascending in a tight corkscrew while spitting out flares from the back. The Taliban's missiles would shoot out of hidden spots on the mountainsides like oversized bottle rockets, tracing a fiery arc through the pale-blue sky, and then usually would get distracted by one of the flares, thus missing the plane. Usually. It's quite a sight if you're safely observing from the ground. Not so pretty if you're in the plane.

It was my first flight out of Kabul, and since I was the only woman on board, the pilot and copilot let me sit in a spare seat in the cockpit. There are no other windows on military transport planes. I thought they were doing me a courtesy. It turned out that courtesy was a form of hazing.

As we trundled down the runway, I realized that every Taliban in those mountains with a missile handy was smiling and gauging our trajectory. Not a comfortable feeling.

"Here we go," the pilot said. "Hold on to your panties."

Sexist commentary was so common in the armed forces, I almost didn't hear him.

Far sooner than I thought he would, the pilot yanked on the controls, and we shot into the air. He almost did it too soon, and we dropped, with a sickening lurch, within a few yards of the tarmac.

But then the plane got the wind beneath its wings, and up we went, twisting and rising, the sun dazzling my eyes and spinning around in my vision. How the pilot saw what he was doing, I have no idea.

To avoid being blinded, I looked to the side just in time to see the first of the Stingers shooting straight for us.

I almost let out a yelp, but the panties comment made me keep my cool, at least externally.

"Incoming," I said in as calm a voice as I could muster.

"There always is," the pilot said.

The copilot chimed in. "If Mitch and I both get killed, do you think you could land this thing?"

"No sweat. How hard could it be?" I replied.

The Stinger was getting closer by the second. With us corkscrewing into the sky, I only got to see it for a couple of seconds at every turn. The pilot and copilot didn't even look at it.

The next time it spun into view, it was almost on

us, and I saw three more in the background, heading our way.

The missiles spun out of sight, and I laid even odds on us blowing up before we turned enough for me to see them again.

We did turn, but I did not see the first one, only the later three.

Then I realized why. The copilot with the bad sense of humor was hitting a button marked FLARES faster than a kid about to beat the high score on an arcade game.

The missile had gotten distracted, or we had flown out of its trajectory, or something. Whatever happened, we were still alive.

"Keep pushing that button," I said.

He stopped pressing it. "What button?"

"That button!"

He looked confused. The remaining three Stingers shot closer.

"Which button?" he asked, indicating a panel full of buttons.

"The one marked FLARES, you idiot!"

He put on a dumb face. "I can't read. I'm too much of an idiot."

I said several unladylike, unprintable things and

started jabbing at that button faster than a kid about to ... well, you know.

The pilot and copilot cackled with laughter. Mitch, the pilot, still corkscrewing the plane into the air, pulled out a fifth of whiskey, opened it with his teeth, and took a swig before handing it to his copilot. The copilot took an even bigger swig and handed it to me.

"Stop screwing around, and get us out of here!" I shouted.

"Stop wasting flares," the pilot said.

He leveled out. I peeked down and saw the last Stinger pass harmlessly below us.

I cheered. The pilot and copilot cheered. We finished the whiskey and cheered some more. Then I shared some breath mints in case an officer came into the cockpit.

So I do cheer on occasion, but it usually takes a lot more than pulling out of port on a floating hotel filled with senior citizens.

It took me a moment to figure out why I was cheering. It wasn't that everyone around me was cheering. I'm not one of the herd. After all, on the gangway, everyone had been complaining, and I had decided to do something more positive, not to mention more useful. No, what I was cheering about was that I had realized I was at a new beginning.

At seventy-one, with a wonderful husband passed away and an exciting career over, I was starting a new life. I had a fine boyfriend, a lovely family, a fair semblance of health, and plenty of years ahead of me to do whatever I wanted.

After James passed, I felt directionless. Retiring had been a hard knock. We had both been devoted to our careers in the CIA, but we had each other, and so we pushed on. Then he had died of a sudden heart attack. After all those gunfights, all those terrifying situations in war zones the general public hadn't even heard of, he had been struck down by the most common of all causes. It had taken a few years for me to finally get my life back together. Moving to Cheerville to be with my family had been the first step. Making friends was an important second step. Joining a gym and regaining some of my fitness was the third.

And now, I realized, being with Octavian was the final step.

As everyone cheered and waved at the indifferent longshoremen on the pier, I turned and gave Octavian our first full kiss on the lips.

Octavian embraced me, and I discovered that he

was quite the kisser. Such a good kisser that my ears started ringing.

Oh, wait, that was from the loud cheers all around us.

I had forgotten about Georgina Branch and her followers. They were cheering us.

We looked at them, slightly flustered, but we didn't let go of each other.

The ship sailed out of port, and we breathed in the fresh sea air. It seemed like we were sailing into calm, sunny waters, and nothing, absolutely nothing, could possibly go wrong.

If only.

FOUR

Things started going wrong only a few minutes after we left port.

We were still on deck, and Georgina was busy organizing everyone's holiday, picking out all sorts of activities for us to do. They were a few years younger than we were but at about the same level of fitness and decided that the morning yoga session would be a good start to the day. When Octavian mentioned he did yoga three times a week, Georgina felt vindicated. Then there was salsa dancing and swimming and the nightly concerts by Tony Iron and the Bar Belles, and once we got down to the islands, there would be plenty of shore trips. It looked like Georgina had our entire trip planned for us.

I'd always rankled under that sort of treatment.

Orders from a superior officer were one thing, but having some pushy alpha female in a seniors' social circle trying to run every moment of our lives was quite another. The thing was, all her ideas were good ones, and she was one of those instantly likeable people who was easy to follow. Feeling giddy from the discovery of Octavian's skill at kissing made me pretty easygoing too.

The easygoing atmosphere disappeared with the snarling words, "Well, well, well, if it isn't Georgina Branch issuing orders again!"

We turned. Standing nearby was a woman of about our age, hands on hips, frown on face, venom on lips. She was remarkable for two things—her height and her terrible fashion sense. She stood six feet four inches and had a heavy frame. I don't mean this as a euphemism for being fat. She was more bulky and broad shouldered than overweight. I suspected she had been an athlete in her younger years. Although it wasn't easy to tell, considering what she was wearing. She had on a shapeless denim dress that looked like a tent on her.

Georgina smiled. "Hello, Maggie. Fancy meeting you here! I didn't know you were coming on this cruise."

"Like hell you didn't."

Georgina looked shocked. "Don't blaspheme. You know it offends Charlotte."

I didn't know who Charlotte was. I supposed she was one of Georgina's coterie. I still hadn't learned the names of all these people.

"You knew very well I was on this cruise," Maggie said. "That's why you booked it—to ruin my vacation just like you ruined my life!"

"Nonsense," Georgina said. "Why would your vacation be of any importance to me?"

Maggie reddened. She turned to us.

"So, I see Georgina has a couple of new recruits. Has she managed to destroy your happiness yet?"

"Um ..." Octavian and I said in unison. We were still arm in arm. What does one say when someone asks you that after the first passionate kiss of your relationship?

"That's enough!" Georgina shouted. "You're not welcome here, Maggie."

At that point everyone started shouting at the same time, even the usually silent Georgina followers.

"This is our cue to leave," Octavian said quietly into my ear.

"Oh yes," I said loudly enough for people to hear. "I almost forgot. We need to talk to the bursar."

"Oh right, the bursar. Let's go," Octavian said.

No one paid us the least attention. We moved along the deck through the crowd, still hearing the sounds of the argument behind us, and headed inside.

"Whew! What was all that about?" I asked.

"I don't know. I'm still trying to figure out what a bursar does."

"It's the person who controls money on the ship. He's like a paymaster."

"Oh. Why would we need to see him?"

"Because he got us out of there."

"Good man. I'll buy him a drink the next time I see him," Octavian said. He stopped and turned to me, his hands on my shoulders. "I'm so happy you said yes to this cruise."

I smiled. "I'm happy I came."

"Promise me one thing."

"What's that?"

"Don't let anyone get murdered. People are always getting murdered around you. It's invigorating, I'll admit, but I'd rather have a relaxing vacation."

"But I'm not the one doing the murdering."

A couple passing by glanced at us curiously.

"True, but the death rate around you is truly

astonishing. That's one of the reasons I asked you along. I was worried Cheerville was in danger of getting depopulated."

"All right, no murders."

Octavian looked relieved. "Good. Let's get something to eat. There's a twenty-four-hour buffet."

"Sounds dangerous."

"With you around, it probably is."

We had a lovely lunch and then wandered around the ship. Octavian had been on many cruises, but this was my first, so I was curious about my new surroundings. Blame my situational awareness, but I spent just as much time looking at fire-escape plans and wondering about unmarked doors as I did admiring the view out the portholes or being impressed by the facilities.

And impressive they were. The casino looked like a smaller version of any of the top-money vampires in Las Vegas. The restaurant where we made our dinner reservations boasted a Michelin rating. The pool was huge, and there were several heart-shaped Jacuzzis. I saw Octavian looking at them speculatively.

After exploring the superstructure, we delved into the lower decks. I could tell Octavian wasn't interested in this part, but he knew I was curious. As we wandered around the maze of hallways and stairs, he commented, "This ship is only about half-full."

"Really? It seems pretty crowded to me."

"Most of these doors don't have a 'do not disturb' sign or 'room service' sign hanging from the knob."

"Hmmm, good point. You're turning into quite the detective."

Octavian smiled. A man is never too old to have his ego stroked.

After a while, we went back up on deck to enjoy the view. The shore had dwindled to a distant line, and ahead of us stretched only sea. The deck wasn't as crowded as before, although there was a keen game of shuffleboard going on. I saw money changing hands.

"Want to play?" Octavian asked.

"No."

Octavian was a bit of a gambler. I didn't like this aspect of his personality, but there were worse vices.

"That's all right, neither do I. Look how they're arguing about who scored what. I'm not partial to seniors' cruises per se, but the all-ages cruises tend to get too many loud drunks and even louder children. That's worse than crabby arguments over shuffle-board any day."

"A penny for your thoughts, and a nickel for using 'per se' in casual conversation."

We spent the afternoon sunning ourselves on deck and drinking cocktails served by white-uniformed waiters who somehow knew the precise moment to ask if we wanted refills and otherwise left us alone. This whole cruise thing wasn't so bad. I could get used to this.

Things took a downturn at dinner. The maître d' took a look at our names and said, "Your group has already arrived. Let me show you to your table."

Somewhat confused, we followed.

He took us straight to a table with Georgina and her gang.

Georgina stood and waggled a wine glass over her head as we approached.

"Yoo-hoo! Over here. So glad you could make it. Now the B Deck, Hall 5 gang is all here!"

"Quite the coincidence that we ended up at the same table," Octavian said, his tone showing he didn't think it was a coincidence at all.

"We looked you up and arranged for you to sit with us for the whole trip. Isn't that nice?" Georgina said.

We sat. I decided to make the best of tonight and fix the situation later.

One of the women filled our wine glasses from a nearly empty bottle. Two other empty bottles stood next to it. A waiter swooped in and delivered another.

The whole table started chattering, and I finally learned everyone's names. There were five women in Georgina's coterie, all recently retired. Charlotte was a retired schoolteacher and an organist at her church. Brenda was a homemaker, as was Alicia. Fiona had worked as an emergency-room nurse, a job that had stressed her out so much she didn't want to talk about it. Lauren had worked as a bookkeeper and was the youngest of the group. The cruise was in celebration of her recent retirement.

"A bookie?" Octavian joked. "Some of my best friends are bookies."

"Oh, a gambling man," Lauren said. "You know I—"

Georgina cut her off. "Lauren once won a thousand dollars in Vegas. We go there sometimes."

"Do you?" Octavian asked while still looking at Lauren, a polite way of keeping her in a conversation from which she had just been ejected.

But Georgina proved unstoppable.

"Oh, sure," she said, refilling Octavian's wine glass even though he hadn't finished it. "We didn't go so much when we were still burdened with jobs and husbands. Now that Lauren has retired, we're all free at last," Georgina said. She had been cutting into all the conversations, and I actually learned more about the other five women from her than from the women themselves.

"It was such a good idea to do this cruise," Lauren said to Georgina. "Thank you so much for coming up with it and organizing everything."

"We girls have to stick together," Georgina said then focused on Octavian and me, leaning forward a little. "So, what's the story with you two lovebirds? Recently married?"

Octavian actually blushed at that. I probably did too.

"No. We've been dating for a few months now, and Octavian surprised me with a cruise."

"As long as he doesn't use it as an excuse to pop the question," Georgina said, waggling a finger at me. "Marriage is always a bad idea. It's better to stay free."

The temperature on our side of the table plunged several degrees. That's not the sort of thing you should say to two widows.

Georgina seemed oblivious to our reaction. She launched into a long, rambling story about how she divorced her husband fifteen years ago, took him for all he had, and never looked back. I gathered from the pained expressions of a couple of her crowd that not everyone agreed that marriage was a bad institution, not that any of them spoke up. I didn't either. It was impossible to get a word in edgewise with someone as in love with the sound of her own voice as Georgina. Besides, I was busy thinking up exit strategies.

Easier said than done. We had barely finished the appetizer, and the main course was slow in coming. More wine appeared. We couldn't take a sip without more being poured into our glasses. Combined with the cocktails we had earlier, I was getting a bit woozy. And that wasn't the worst of it. Octavian and I had to endure endless gossip about various people we didn't know. Georgina was the main perpetrator, although her little band piped up as much as they could, looking for approval.

Surprisingly, no one mentioned Maggie, the woman they had a fight with on deck. I figured she would be the main target of their spite.

At last we got through dessert, and Octavian leaped up with an excuse on his lips about how we had to check on something.

"But we were going to order shots," Georgina

said. "I've heard they have a lemon liqueur to die for. It's from Italy."

"Ah yes, limoncello," he said, pronouncing it perfectly. "I used to order it in Tuscany."

"Then you'll want to stay."

"No, we really must go," Octavian said. "We'll have to talk about Tuscany sometime. The people there have so much culture."

Did I hear the faintest stress on the word "culture"? Georgina obviously did not. She put on a pouty face and said, "Oh, all right. We'll let you go this time, but don't you dare pop the question."

"What an insufferable gaggle of poisonous geese," Octavian grumbled as soon as we were out of earshot.

"I didn't know geese could be poisonous, but I agree," I replied.

"How about you commit a few murders instead of solving them?"

"Tempted."

"Shall we go up on deck to get some fresh air?"

"I think we both need it."

The sun had already set, and we stepped out into a dark night under a canopy of brilliant stars. A few others were out admiring the night, too, although not as many as one would think. The thudding of classic rock from the direction of the disco told us that some people were trying to relive their youth, and I was sure the casino was doing good business as well.

I preferred it out here, arm in arm with a dapper gentleman, far away from the noise and gossip of the seniors' cruise.

We fell into a companionable silence, strolling along in the subdued light of the deck, admiring the stars and listening to the low thrum of the engine and the water splashing against the prow.

I turned to kiss Octavian and found him already moving in.

We had another kiss on the lips, enjoyed all the more for the lack of an audience.

There was a scream from farther away on deck, followed by a splash. Then came another couple of screams.

Octavian rolled his eyes. "You've done it again."

"Someone's fallen overboard!" a male voice shouted.

"More likely pushed, knowing you," Octavian grumbled. We were already running for the source of the sound. Well, more of a brisk walk. Running was not my forte anymore, and it wasn't Octavian's either.

The sounds led us to the prow, where a small

crowd stood peering over the edge. Someone was shouting into a red emergency phone. There were several all along the deck in case of an accident.

"And now she's in the water! Stop the boat!"

"What happened?" I asked.

A woman at the railing turned to me. "Someone was standing on the prow, doing a *Titanic* imitation. You know, with her arms up in the air and facing the wind. Then she fell in."

I glanced at the prow. The chain that sealed it off had been unhooked. The warning sign that hung from it now lay on the deck.

"How did she fall in?" I asked, peering over the side and not seeing any sign of the victim.

"I don't know. We just passed by and saw her. As we went around the corner, we heard her scream. Then we came back, and she was gone."

"She must have killed herself," one of the men said.

Maybe. But if someone was determined to kill herself, she probably wouldn't scream on the way down.

Some sailors and a couple of waiters came rushing out, and the whole conversation was repeated. A minute later, floodlights lit up the entire exterior. Several people on deck complained it was ruining their view but shut up quickly as the news spread. Contrary to popular belief, there is a limit to what a senior citizen will complain about.

I stayed put by the prow, listening in as a manager asked the group about the woman who had fallen in.

"Did she say anything to you?" the manager asked.

"Nothing. I don't think she even saw us. She was facing out to sea with her arms upraised."

"Inside or outside the railing?"

"Inside. I didn't think she was going to jump."

"What did she look like?"

"Very tall. Bulky too. Big woman. She was wearing a denim dress."

Octavian and I glanced at each other. Maggie, the woman who had been arguing with Georgina and her crew. I couldn't imagine anyone else would fit that description.

The boat engine went into reverse and brought the boat to a stop, then cut off entirely. Searchlights scanned the surrounding water. A couple of lifeboats crewed by sailors were lowered. By now a large crowd stood on deck, trading the news and looking down into the water. A couple of unhelpful people pointed to every shadow caused by a wave and shouted, "There she is! There she is!"

"What do you think?" Octavian asked in a low voice.

"I'm thinking what you're thinking. Maggie might not have jumped. She might have been pushed."

We tried to go to the tip of the prow, where she had stood, but a sailor had already replaced the chain and was standing guard. Another sailor stood at the prow where Maggie had been standing, gripping the railing and looking down, as if she would still be there, hanging on to the bulkhead or something. Several people milled around. If there had been any evidence at the scene, it was long gone now.

Directly opposite the prow stood the very front of the ship's superstructure. The first floor was only twenty or so yards from the tip of the prow. Above this first floor, the upper levels stepped back, becoming smaller with each level until they ended in a high radio and radar tower. On the deck level, there was a glassed-in viewing deck for people who wanted to see the sea while remaining out of the elements. All lights were blazing inside, and at least a dozen people stood in there, yammering about the accident.

I thought for a moment.

"Were these lights on when we heard the splash?" I asked Octavian.

"Not all of them. Remember how they only had a couple of dim lights burning in the outer rooms so it would be dark on deck? I guess they did that so we could admire the stars."

"So this room was fairly dark and full of shadows —" I said.

Octavian finished. "And the murderer could have gone out that door directly behind the prow, snuck up on Maggie, and pushed her in ..."

"The murderer could have been waiting for the right moment," I went on. "Looking out these windows, he or she would have seen the group of people pass by. They were probably talking and looking at the stars and wouldn't have noticed someone standing still in the shadows. As soon as they disappeared around the corner, the murderer could have snuck up and pushed Maggie over the edge—"

"And then made their escape back into here, through that door in the back wall, and then anywhere on the ship they wanted to go."

Octavian and I stared at each other for a moment.

"We have another murder on our hands," I said.

"I should have known I'd never get a peaceful vacation with you along."

I grinned. Octavian shook his head ruefully and grinned back.

"Let's go check on Georgina and her friends."

FIVE

We went down to the dining room and found them gone. I asked our waiter when they had left, and he shrugged his shoulders.

"About half an hour ago, I suppose."

Not long after we left.

"Did they say where they were going?" Octavian asked.

"No, sir."

We went around the entire deck and saw no sign of them. That was a bit suspicious because it seemed like almost everyone was on deck, staring out at the unfolding drama in the sea. A couple of Coast Guard helicopters had arrived from shore and were circling around, adding their spotlights to those from the lifeboats and the ship itself.

It was all necessary and according to procedure but unlikely to be successful. The deck was as high above the surface of the water as a four-story building. Falling from that height, the impact with the water was enough to knock most people out. Falling right at the prow, the body would likely be sucked under the ship. Even if Maggie had somehow survived that, it had been more than half an hour since she had fallen in. I doubted someone her age, having undergone such a shock, would be able to tread water for half an hour.

But the Coast Guard weren't the kind of people to give up. I knew a few of them in my time, when we did joint operations to intercept major drug shipments, and they were tenacious. They did not give up the search until well beyond the point where all hope was lost.

Leaving the ship's crew and the Coast Guard to their sad, hopeless task, we went back inside and searched the observation decks, the casino, the nightclub, and all three bars.

Not a sign of them.

"They're hiding in their cabins," Octavian said.

"Possibly."

"They're guilty as hell."

"Probably. At least one of them is."

"Probably more than one," Octavian said. "Did you see how big Maggie was? I'm not sure Georgina or one of the others could have pushed her over, even with the element of surprise."

Awww, he said "element of surprise." He was really getting into this sleuthing thing, wasn't he?

He also had a good point.

"If they were planning a murder, why would they invite us to their table?" I asked.

Octavian rubbed his chin. "I'm not sure. And they didn't invite us. They actually forced us to sit at their table."

"Georgina did. Georgina runs the show with that crowd."

"So maybe Georgina didn't do it. Maybe it was one or more of her flunkies."

"And now they've all disappeared," I said, looking around the lounge where we sat, hoping we would be lucky enough for them to walk in. "They must have heard the news by now."

"They're probably in one of their cabins talking about it, the guilty ones keeping up appearances."

We lapsed into silence. The murderers hadn't had much time to go up and lie in wait for Maggie after we left. They must have left right after we did and known she was going up there at around that time. But how could they have known that? It didn't seem like Maggie would have told them. They weren't on speaking terms as far as I could see.

If only we knew more about what that big blowup on deck had been about. Maggie had said something about Georgina and her crowd ruining her life and that they had deliberately come on this cruise to ruin her vacation. That implied they knew she was coming even though they weren't on speaking terms. Odd.

Maybe the rumor mill back home told them? But where was back home? And what relationship did these people have with Maggie? I knew virtually nothing about any of these people. I didn't even know their last names.

Perhaps I was making something out of nothing. I'd been surrounded by death so long, I'd come to suspect everyone and everything. Maybe Maggie really did jump. She said her life was ruined after all.

But that didn't sit well with me. It was too pat, too easy. If she wanted to jump, she would have reacted to the crowd coming into view, not just ignored them. She would have stepped back, acted casual, like people do when they're caught about to do something that others would stop them from doing.

And the witnesses said she was standing inside the railing. She hadn't gotten onto the outside and stood there, gripping the railing, trying to summon up her courage like a jumper would.

This was all too hypothetical. I needed more information.

"Let's take another look at the prow," I said.

"All right," Octavian said with a resigned sigh. This was not how he had envisioned our vacation.

There was less of a crowd on deck than before. The evening breeze had grown cooler, and that mixed with the boredom of seeing nothing happen with the rescue operation had made many head inside to resume their drinking, dancing, and gambling. My heart sank. Maggie was already becoming yesterday's news.

Not to the Coast Guard and the crew. They were still out there, scouring the sea with their searchlights. It had been well over an hour now, and I could see there was no hope.

First, we went to the observation deck behind the prow. A few people still sat in there, talking about what had happened. From what I eavesdropped, I could tell everyone assumed it had been a suicide.

"Poor woman. She should have talked to some-one," a woman in her eighties said, sitting in a little circle of similarly aged people. All tut-tutted and shook their heads.

"Oh yes. When I'm feeling blue, I always talk to my cats. Did I tell you about my cats? I have fifteen of them. There's Chester and Linus and ..."

"You would think she would kill herself some-where else and not inconvenience everyone."

"And Mildred and Ethel ..."

"At least she didn't throw herself in front of a train. Think of the mess!"

"And Constanze and Abigail ..."

"Yes, that would be terrible, but now we've stopped to look for her, and we'll probably be late getting to the islands."

"And Alphonse and William Shatner ..."

"Why don't they put out some big fishing nets? I'm sure they could find her that way. Get some fresh fish for the buffet too."

"And Abelard and Heloise ..."

"There are no security cameras," Octavian observed.

"No there aren't," I replied. "Let's go out to the prow."

The sailor who had been standing on guard duty

was still at his post. The other one, the one who had been looking over the edge, had left. That made me feel sad. He was the first searcher to give up. Soon the boats would come in, the searchlights from the cruise ship would turn off, and the helicopters would head to shore over a dark sea.

Maggie's body, in all likelihood, would never be found.

We stood at the railing not far from the chained-off area. The guard didn't even look at us.

The railing at the tip of the prow was no higher than it was everywhere else. I gauged the height of the railing compared to myself. I'm five foot five, and the railing was at chest level. With Maggie being a foot taller than me, the railing would have been at her midriff, still above her center of gravity. It would have taken quite a force to tip her over the edge. Perhaps one person pushing while the other grabbed Maggie's legs and lifted?

That would have required some strength. Maggie looked pretty heavy, and they would have had to catch her by surprise, or they would have had a fight on their hands, a fight I couldn't picture Georgina or any of her followers winning. Plus that crowd of witnesses had been so close they would have heard a struggle.

So they had a concrete plan, cooperation, and more importantly, the resolution to carry it out.

This final element is one most people overlook. We can all sit there and think up clever ways to kill people, but getting the will to carry it through with no hesitation and no panicking is the tough part. Summoning that inner evil is a difficult thing, and getting more than one person to do it is even harder. This is what boot camp is for, to train groups of young people to obey orders to kill without thinking about it. Civilians do not have that training and need a lot of motivation to cross that line.

Or the proper leader.

Georgina certainly had a hold on these women.

"Do you suppose they've arranged to sit with us at breakfast too?" I asked.

"Most likely. We'll have to keep our eyes and ears open."

I nodded. It was sure going to be an interesting breakfast.

Octavian and I arranged to meet outside our cabins at nine the following morning. I figured a late breakfast would be a good idea, considering how much that crowd had been knocking back at dinner. And they had probably been up late. No one commits a brazen murder and then turns in early for a good night's sleep.

Well, professional killers did, but I didn't think they were in that category. They didn't have that reptilian look in their eyes.

When Octavian and I met in the hall, none of the other cabin doors were open, and we hadn't heard them come out. After checking the coast was clear, we listened at each cabin door but heard nothing. The doors were pretty thick, so we wouldn't catch anything but loud noises. At least no one was getting murdered in the cabins at that moment. I can't handle murder before breakfast. Shrugging our shoulders, we headed to the restaurant.

An announcement had been posted in all the public rooms. Bordered in black, it regretted to inform us that Margaret Underwood had apparently committed suicide by jumping from the prow last night. An extensive search by the ship's crew and the Coast Guard had failed to find her. Anyone with any information should inform a member of staff immediately. The entire crew of the *Silver Siren* and all the staff and management of Surf n' Sun Cruise Line expressed their heartfelt sympathies, blah blah blah.

It didn't tell us anything we didn't already know.

Even getting there late, we didn't see Georgina

and her followers. We took a slow pass around the extensive restaurant. At least two hundred people were eating there, mostly by the floor-to-ceiling windows that gave a splendid view of the sea. I noticed the ship was moving again.

There were no reserved tables for breakfast, so we got a table near the entrance to catch them when they came in. We ate slowly, scanning the aged crowd. Many looked like they were sporting hangovers. Others were already sunburned. Everyone was talking about their own affairs. I didn't hear a single mention of Maggie.

After sitting there an hour, we were about to give up when we saw them come in.

Georgina came in first, leading the pack, as usual. She was perfectly done up, not a single bottle-blond hair out of place. I did notice a bit of strain around her eyes and a bit of stiffness in her movements. Hungover or feeling guilty? Hard to say. Although given the amount she had drunk at dinner, she must be hungover no matter what else she might be feeling.

The others looked fairly hungover too. They were all perfectly done up, though. Everyone wore bright sundresses like nothing had gone wrong on their holiday at all.

"There are the lovebirds!" Georgina cried when she spotted us. Her face lit up, and she gave us a broad smile. Her followers smiled, too, as if on cue.

They sat down. Georgina fixed me with a sly look and said, "I bet you're wondering about Maggie."

SIX

It took a moment to recover from such a direct statement. I had expected the need to be subtle and slowly bring the conversation around to what had happened the night before. Instead, she had come right out and invited us to talk with her about it.

Before I could respond, she flagged down a waiter and ordered a Bloody Mary. Her followers did too.

"Best thing for a hangover," she said when she turned to us again. "Want one?"

"No thank you. So, what happened last night?" I asked, trying to play the clueless innocent.

Georgina shook her head sadly. Or at least she did a good imitation of sadness. It was hard to tell with her since she was such a show-woman. "Maggie has always been a bit unstable. We all live in the same neighborhood in Schenectady. Of course everyone in the neighborhood socializes with everyone else. That's the kind of community Schenectady is. Unfortunately, that means sometimes you have to deal with people who don't quite fit in."

"Maggie was one of those," Charlotte said.

A flicker of anger passed over Georgina's features, as if she was annoyed by the interruption. Georgina went on. "She never got married, and while I don't generally approve of marriage, it might have done her some good. She worked as a librarian for the Schenectady Municipal Library, shushing everyone who so much as flipped a page loudly. Nobody at work liked her, neither the patrons nor her coworkers, and she was foul tempered and bossy outside of work too."

"Bossiness is a terrible personality trait," Octavian said. I could have kicked him, but Georgina was not the kind of person who caught on to irony.

"It is indeed," she said. "She made enemies all through the neighborhood by sticking her nose into everyone's business. She always thought she knew what was best for everyone and tried to organize everything to her standard."

I stifled a smile. Georgina reminded me of a saying by Benjamin Franklin: "The proud hate pride —in others."

Georgina continued talking. I had only known her a day, and I had already realized that talking was what she did best. "But I'm a charitable sort, and I took her under my wing. It wasn't easy, I tell you, but I invited her along when we had tea at a cafe or we went bowling."

"Bowling?" I had a hard time imagining these people bowling.

"Oh yes, we decided to form our own bowling team last year. Did you know they have bowling lanes right here on board the ship? We'll be bowling later today, once we're feeling a bit better. You should come along."

"But why would she throw herself off the boat?" I asked, still playing the innocent. As I asked this, I glanced around the table and felt like I was in a poker game. Everyone had suddenly gone expressionless. I made a mental note to stay well away from any railings if I was on deck with these people.

Georgina was the only one showing emotion, even if it was fake.

"It's so terrible, isn't it?" she said in a fair imitation of anguish. "What a wasted life. No friends, no lovers. If only she had tried to reach out ..."

"The way she accosted you, it sounded like you used to be in the same social circle," Octavian said.

"Oh, Schenectady is such a small community there really is only one social circle, at least only one worth being in." Her followers tittered. "But Maggie wasn't ever able to fit in. We tried. Lord knows we tried. There's just no helping some people. She made quite a few enemies."

Oh, did she now? That was an odd thing for a suspect to admit.

"Enemies?" I asked. "She seemed harmless enough."

"She held grudges," Lauren said with some heat.

For once, Georgina didn't seem angered at the interruption. She nodded to her and said, "That she did. When she was passed over for promotion at the library in favor of one of her coworkers, she badmouthed the other woman relentlessly. For years! And then there was the bowling fiasco."

"The bowling Armageddon!" Fiona chirped, and the other women tittered.

"Indeed," Georgina said. "As I said, we had invited her along for a couple of our practice sessions, just to be friendly. Well, she was a disaster.

She practically threw the ball into the gutter. When we tried to give her advice, she got all snappy. We tried to be patient and even gave her encouragement. That turned out to be a mistake."

"She got it into her head that she was on the team," Fiona said. "We explained to her that the team was already full, but it didn't sink in."

"Then came our tournament," Charlotte cut in. "We had made it to the finals of the Schenectady Senior Bowling League Golden Trophy Tournament, when I fell ill with a case of malaria."

"Malaria?" Octavian asked, looking at her with astonishment. "I didn't realize Schenectady was in a malarial zone."

I almost kicked him. I didn't want them to get off topic.

"My late husband and I were missionaries in Bangladesh for a few years. I contracted malaria there. You recover, but it stays in your system. Every now and then it comes back. Terrible affliction. I was laid out in bed, sweating gallons of water every hour, just when my team needed me the most!"

Georgina shook her head sadly. "We went to the tournament and pled our case, but the rules were quite strict that we had to have a full team to compete. We got desperate and searched around the bowling center for a pickup player, but everyone was either in another team or rooting for another team. We were at our wits' end. And then Maggie showed up and volunteered. Well, we certainly weren't going to have her on our team. It's one thing to forfeit. Humiliating yourself in front of half of Schenectady is another thing entirely."

"So you refused her?" I asked.

Georgina raised her eyes heavenward. "She was beside herself with rage. She said she had been practicing day and night and that we should give her another chance. Perhaps she had been practicing, but it would have taken three miracles and an executive order from the president to have made her a decent bowler, let alone one who could compete in the Schenectady Senior Bowling League Golden Trophy Tournament."

"A high point in bowling history, to be sure," Octavian said.

This time I did kick him. He let out a little grunt.

"So we said no," Georgina went on, oblivious. "We went up to the judge to announce that we had to forfeit. Just then Charlotte flew in and saved the day."

"More like stumbled in and moaned that she could play," Charlotte corrected.

"And play you did," Georgina said with a smile. "Of course you weren't up to your usual level, but the rest of the team took up the slack, and we got the gold!"

"One for all and all for one, the Six Mouseyke-teers!" they said in unison, bringing their hands together over the table in a communal high five.

Good Lord.

Just then the waiter arrived with the Bloody Marys, and they began to drink in earnest. I decided it was time to withdraw and confer with Octavian.

"So, what do you think?" Octavian asked once we got into the corridor and out of earshot.

"I think we need to get these people alone and talk to them one by one."

"Easier said than done. Georgina rules the roost, and they all follow her wherever she goes."

"True, but I have a hard time believing Maggie killed herself because she was a failure at bowling."

"Bowling is quite important to some people. You're right, though, it's not something to take a swim over. How about we ... what's going on?"

The drone of the engine, a regular background noise all day and night, had shifted. Since the engine was always on, we didn't even notice it most of the time, but now it had changed tone, getting softer, deeper.

"We're slowing down," I said. I'd been on enough Navy ships to know these things.

"But we're in the middle of the sea."

"Let's go on deck and see what's happening."

"Maybe they found Maggie's body."

"That would be a stroke of luck."

We came up on deck to see something unexpected. Not far off the port bow was another cruise ship, smaller than ours. Both it and our own had stopped. Squinting, I could make out the name as the *Poseidon Party*, and beneath the name was Surf n' Sun Cruise Line's logo.

A small crowd had gathered to stare.

"What's going on?" a gray-haired gentleman asked as a sailor passed by.

"Engine trouble with the other ship, sir. We're going to transfer their guests onto our ship and continue the cruise."

"Another delay!" the man exclaimed. "Are we going to get to the islands at all?"

"We'll make it to the islands on schedule, sir," the sailor said, turning and leaving before the gentleman could start griping again.

We watched as the crew of the *Poseidon Party*

lowered their lifeboats and motored on over to us. Each boat was piled high with passengers and their luggage. Thudding electronic music preceded them over the water. Our ship lowered a gangway, and the passengers started coming aboard.

As one lifeboat after another emptied their passengers onto our ship, I noticed a couple of things.

First, most of the passengers were young, tanned, and in great shape.

Secondly, every single one of them was a man.

One particularly tanned and muscular young man, stripped to the waist to show off his impressive pectorals, which gleamed with oil in the Caribbean sun, lowered his sunglasses and surveyed the deck.

"Antoine," he said to the European-looking man standing next to him, who was equally muscular and oiled. "Are we on a ... seniors' cruise?"

"Oh. My. God. I do believe you're right."

The first man looked at Antoine and got a mischievous look in his eye. "Are you thinking what I'm thinking?" he asked.

Antoine gave him a sultry smile. "I do believe I am. Let's cause some heart attacks."

They embraced and locked lips. One of the old women shrieked. The elderly gentleman who had been complaining about the delay shouted, "Good Lord!" and stomped off the deck.

Another muscled and oiled twentysomething came on deck, pumped his fist in the air, and shouted. "Come on, girls. It's time to parteeeeey!"

Octavian looked on, aghast. "Did we just get invaded by a … gay cruise?"

"Yes," I said as the deck began to fill with dancing, flirting, and singing young men. "Yes, we did."

SEVEN

It's times like these where you really get to know people. As the senior citizens left the deck in droves, Octavian surveyed the new crowd, shrugged his shoulders, and said, "Oh well, I didn't really want to go to the disco anyway. So how are we going to handle the investigation?"

"We have to break up Georgina's group somehow and isolate each person," I said, relieved Octavian wasn't going into conniptions over our new shipmates like some of the senior citizens on deck. In fact, they were fleeing en masse. So were the sailors. The new passengers found their uniforms fetching and were trying to fetch the men inside them. Within moments we were alone on deck with a rapidly growing crowd of gay men a third our age.

"Let's check out that bowling alley," Octavian said. "Maybe they'll be there already."

It turned out they were. The bowling alley was on one of the lowest decks and was fitted out with six lanes. We had to check our shoes and each rent a pair of those embarrassingly ugly shoes bowling alleys always give out. Once inside, we spotted them at one of the lanes. Only one other lane was taken, by a husband and wife who were keeping to themselves.

Georgina and her gang were all drunk again, their hangovers forgotten in a pleasant alcoholic fog of Bloody Marys. And I must say that the Six Mouseyketeers lived up to their boasts. One by one, in rapid succession, they went up and got strikes or at least spares. Bowling pins flew in all directions.

The accuracy and force with which they launched their bowling balls was frightening. Looking for comparison at the husband and wife a couple of lanes away, who struggled up to the line to practically drop their balls to send them sedately toward the pins, I could see just how skilled the Six Mouseyketeers were. No wonder they had won the gold. They were shooting their personalized bowling balls down that lane like they were firing them from a cannon.

And that got me thinking. I hadn't quite formulated my thoughts when they spotted us.

"Octavian! Barbara! Glad you could join us!" Georgina said, slurring her words slightly. The alcohol content in her blood didn't stop her from turning and making a perfect strike.

"I don't think we're at your level," Octavian said. "We'll get our own lane next to yours. Would you be so kind as to send over one of the Six Mouseyketeers to give us a few tips?"

What a helpful man. He'd figured out the perfect way to isolate a member of the team. They sent over Lauren, the retired bookkeeper whose retirement they had taken a cruise to celebrate. I had noticed her giving Octavian the eye earlier. I didn't think he noticed, which was just fine by me. He was not supposed to notice such things. I suspected her being chosen as our teacher wasn't a coincidence.

Octavian picked up a bowling ball and approached the line.

"Oh, wait! That's not the way," Lauren said. "Here, let me help with your form."

As I watched, she adjusted his hips, her hands far lower than they needed to be.

"That's right. Now square your shoulders like

so." Her hands ran up his chest to move his shoulders into position.

I looked on, appalled, as Lauren fondled my boyfriend. Octavian looked uncomfortable, but he stayed in character, smiling at her and asking her all sorts of technical questions about the "sport and art of bowling."

I kept reminding myself that he was doing this for the sake of the case. Seeing the rest of the Six Mouseyketeers leering at them from the other lane did not help matters.

Finally, he threw the darned ball and took out six pins. Lauren gave him some more hands-on instructions, and he picked up the spare.

"Very good," she said, squeezing his shoulder. "Ooh, you have some strength. I see you work out."

"Seniors' yoga three times a week, and I go power walking on off days," Octavian said with pride.

I fumed and selected a ball.

When it came to be my turn, Lauren motioned to me from several steps away.

"Now just do it like I showed Octavian."

No hands-on instruction for me. I let loose, and it went straight into the gutter. My second ball only took out three pins.

"Don't worry. You'll get the hang of it," Lauren

said. She turned back to Octavian. "So where did you say you live again?"

"Cheerville."

"I've never heard of it."

"There's no reason why you would have. You're a good teacher. Why couldn't you get Maggie up to the mark?"

Lauren gave a sly look at the Six Mouseyketeers, who had stopped watching her poach my boyfriend and were huddled around the scorecard.

"Oh, she wasn't as hopeless a bowler as Georgina lets on. She wasn't at our level, mind you, but she sure was competition in other matters."

"How so?" Octavian asked.

Lauren was about to speak, but then her eyes went wide, and she looked beyond us. "What are they doing here?"

Two of our new shipmates had come in, all golden tans and coifed hair.

"Oh, a gay cruise ship had some engine trouble, so they're joining our cruise," Octavian said.

"Hi, Grandpa!" one of them called to Octavian and waved. "Seven girls all to yourself. Why you randy old man!"

Octavian blushed.

"He only gets one of us!" Lauren called back with a grin.

"Indeed he does," I growled. I knew I shouldn't have been alienating a witness (or suspect), but it just came out.

The two young men sauntered over to the lane next to us.

"These shoes are horrid," one complained. "Why can't they make bowling shoes that look fetching? And they squeak when I walk. I sound like a mattress in a cheap motel."

"The balls are nice, though," his friend said, holding up a pair.

They both started tittering.

"Disgusting!" Georgina snapped. "Girls, let's go."

Lauren went pale and hurried over to her friends, and they tromped out, noses in the air. Each carried her own bowling ball except for Alicia.

"Bye, ladies!" the man who had complained about the shoes cried in a singsong voice, wiggling his fingers in the air.

The couple at the other lane made their escape too.

He turned to us.

"Why haven't you two fled with the rest?" he asked.

I studied him a moment. "Young man, I may not look like it now, but I was in the armed forces for thirty years. You can't shock me."

I could see in his eyes that he didn't believe a word I said. He gave me a mock salute then dove in and gave his companion a long French kiss.

When they came up for air, they saw us doing the same.

"Augh!" they cried in unison and fled for the door, their ugly bowling shoes squeaking furiously.

Octavian and I laughed.

"That was nice," my boyfriend said. "We should shock the young more often."

We finished our game in the now-abandoned bowling alley and took a stroll, arm in arm, around the ship.

It had changed character completely. The three different bars had turned from places of quiet conversation to loud parties. The pool was full of bronzed bodies doing back flips or splashing about and laughing, and the casino was packed.

"Finally, this ship has a bit of life to it," Octavian said.

"I thought you liked seniors' cruises because they were quieter."

"Yes, but I like seeing stodgy old people getting offended even more."

He had a point. Most of the seniors had retreated to their cabins or those last bastions of the older generation —the shuffleboard court and the bingo hall. No young gay man had stepped foot in either of them. I wondered if elderly gay men played shuffleboard or bingo. Gay people are allowed to be boring, too, aren't they?

We didn't see Georgina or her friends anywhere, so we guessed they had gone to their cabins like so many others.

"Let's split up," Octavian said. "We can cover more ground that way."

"In horror movies, that always leads to someone getting gruesomely killed," I replied.

"But this isn't a horror movie."

"Maggie was murdered."

Octavian grew serious. "All the more reason to get cracking. I'll go knock on one of the cabins and have a chat. Maybe I can find out something more."

"Avoid Lauren."

"A potential murderer is no competition for you, pretty lady. They see you as competition, though, and will open up more if you're not around. Why don't you sneak around and see what you can find elsewhere? We'll meet in a bit."

"All right."

I wasn't sure what "sneaking around" would accomplish, so I returned to my cabin to use my phone without any disturbance from the party I could hear echoing down the corridors. Like a good detective in the cyber age, I did some Internet research on Maggie. It wasn't hard to find a librarian in Schenectady. Margaret Underwood had very little in the way of an online footprint, even for someone of our age. There was a short article in the library newsletter about her retirement but no mention of her in any previous newsletters. No mention of any awards or commendations either. She appeared to have had an unremarkable career.

She did have a social media presence, but an odd and profoundly sad one. Her Facebook page was public, and once I made an account for myself, I could see everything. I was surprised to see she had 942 friends. As I scrolled down, I saw that none of them appeared to be actual friends, but random people she chatted with. It said, "Friend me and I'll follow back" right on her bio.

I'd heard of this, people getting on Facebook and

following anybody and everybody in order to bump up the numbers. I didn't get it. Wouldn't having almost a thousand nonfriends make you feel more alone than not having social media at all?

Looking through her status updates, a few things did catch my interest.

The first was a photo of our cruise ship taken from the pier, dated to the day we set sail. The caption said, "My second cruise, and my first without you. At 9:17 tonight I will do what we once did together. Our special time. You may be far away, but you are still in my heart."

Nine seventeen p.m. was roughly the time that Maggie got murdered.

Farther down, in earlier posts, there were some selfies of her bowling with a bunch of people I didn't recognize from a group called the Schenectady Bowlers' Meetup. They all had those plastered smiles of fake fun that made me suspect this was some sort of organized social event rather than a group of real friends. There were also photos of her cats and gerbils, way too many of those, and photos of sunsets and birds in her little garden. Yes, this was definitely a lonely woman.

But then, in a series of status updates from six

months before, I came across some images that were of an entirely different nature.

I knew I was onto something when I saw a close-up of Maggie in some restaurant. She was beaming at the camera, looking truly happy instead of wearing a pasted-on smile. I found myself smiling back at her. To see someone who had had such a gray, unhappy life looking so at peace and joyful for a change was truly heart-warming.

The next picture told me why. It showed her hugging a man around her age. Both were smiling at the camera, standing on a pier at the seaside somewhere.

The catty side of me noticed that this man was not what you'd call a prize catch. He needed badly a gym membership and a fashion makeover. He looked as dull and conventional as Maggie. As big and bulky too.

But they were obviously in love. I could see that from the next several pictures. Them at the beach. Them at a theater. Them smooching in front of a statue of Jimmy Carter.

Jimmy Carter? With a bit of Googling, I discovered he had briefly lived in Schenectady while he was a student. I never thought of Jimmy Carter as a particularly romantic personage, but these two love-birds obviously did.

Actually they probably didn't care. You could have set them in front of a statue of a cow patty at the Kansas State Fair, and they would have still snuggled and smooched.

Then came several photos of them on a cruise ship—playing shuffleboard, eating at a buffet, watching a sunset, and doing an imitation of the scene from *Titanic* on the prow, him behind her, both with their arms upraised and looking forward as the ship hove through the waves.

The time stamp for that shot was 9:17 PM.

The night she embarked on our cruise, she wrote how she would relive that happy moment and give anyone who looked at this public profile her exact whereabouts and the time she'd be there.

After a few more shots back in Schenectady, there were no more pictures of the mystery man, who the status updates named only as Wesley. Previous shots were the same dreary collection as those that came later. Judging from her Facebook, Wesley had swept her off her feet about eight months ago and disappeared from the scene six months ago.

Two months. Two months of happiness. That's all she got. I felt like crying.

I searched for Wesley on Facebook, and it looked like he didn't have an account. He wasn't tagged in any of the photos, and he had never commented on any of her status updates.

Or maybe he had unfriended her. Oh dear, that would be even worse. Finally finding someone and being cut out. Losing the one real friend she had out of nearly a thousand fake ones. What a waste.

I stared at my phone, distraught. I had gone through a long period of self-pity when my husband, James, had died. In the blackest periods, I had felt like I was alone in the world, although I knew in my heart that wasn't true. I had my family. There was no mention of family in Maggie's Facebook. I had friends, too, real ones. I had all those things we take for granted on a day-to-day basis but which are vital to living a healthy, full life. Having those things helps pull you out of the bad times. They sure helped pull me out of my period of mourning.

But who was there to help Maggie? No one.

Maybe she really did throw herself off the boat.

A knock at the door woke me out of my reverie. I opened it. Octavian walked in and slammed the door behind him. He looked furious. Octavian was normally so placid, so friendly to everyone. It was strange to see him red with rage.

"What happened?" I asked.

"What a nest of vipers! Those drug traffickers and dictators you used to go after were probably better people."

"What happened?"

"I didn't know who was in which cabin, so I just knocked on a random one in this wing. They've taken over all of them like some cancerous growth. It turned out to be Brenda and Charlotte's cabin. They were in there, drinking of course. That seems to be all these people do, that and spit venom. Well, they sat me down and poured me a tall one and then started bashing you."

"Me?"

"Oh yes. I won't even repeat the things they said about you. They went on and on, and I noticed Brenda sending a text. She tried to hide her phone behind her, but I saw. And guess who showed up a minute later?"

"Lauren."

"That's right. And the instant she arrived, the other two made an excuse to leave."

"Uh-oh."

"No prizes for guessing what happened next." He paced back and forth, seething. This being a cabin on a ship, he only got to take three steps in any one direction before he had to turn around, and he was walking so fast it made him look like a spinning top. I started to giggle.

"I fail to see why this is so funny," Octavian growled.

I pinched him on the cheek. "Because you are such a gentleman. Fending off the ladies to be true to your girlfriend. It's adorable."

"It was sickening, adult women acting like catty little middle schoolers. And a waste of time too! I learned nothing from any of them."

"Oh, Octavian, that's where you're wrong."

He stopped and looked at me. "How?"

I showed him Maggie's Facebook feed. Realization dawned on his face.

"Oh. That poor woman. One of them poached this Wesley fellow. No wonder she said they had ruined her life. They really did. I bet they didn't even want him. I bet they did it out of pure spite and malice."

I nodded. "Do you think Maggie really did kill herself?"

He rubbed his chin. "Maybe, but did you see how they all got tense and defensive when you talked about her suicide? Everyone but Georgina, that is. My gut tells me one of them pushed her."

"My gut says the same thing."

"And your gut is far more experienced than mine."

"Don't underestimate your gut, Octavian. I think quite highly of your gut."

"And I hate their guts," Octavian said with more heat than I'd ever heard from him. "Let's find out who did it and nail them. But how?"

"We've found their weakness. They're so toxic they go after anyone who looks happy."

"As a salve for their own unhappiness. But I fail to see how we can exploit this to find the murderer."

I pinched his cheek again. "That's because you're a good man. If you want to fight evil people, you have to think like an evil person. It's not pretty, but there it is. So here's what we're going to do ..."

EIGHT

After a long conference with Octavian, in which it took a great deal of convincing to bring the old dear around to my way of thinking, we dug some more on the Internet for information about Maggie, found nothing, and then tried to look up Georgina and the others. We found virtually nothing on any of them. We didn't know any of their last names, so we had to scan through various pages of information on their hometown. All we got was a mention of their bowling team, which did not list the members and therefore didn't help us find their full names. We needed to find those out if we were going to do any digging on these people.

At last we gave up and went to dinner. I was surprised at how late it had already become.

Tracking down a killer always made the clock speed up. What's the old saying? Time flies when you're having fun.

Octavian was having less fun. He was not happy with his role in this investigation. And he was bound to get a lot less happy.

When we arrived at the main dining room, we discovered we were still at Georgina's table. I got the impression she was almost relieved when we showed up, and she immediately brought us into the conversation by asking mock scandalous questions about what Octavian and I had been doing. Lauren looked unsettled, as did some of the others. If Lauren was trying to steal Octavian from me, she obviously hadn't gotten Georgina on her side.

That was odd, considering how much of a ringleader Georgina was and how the day before she had been leering with the rest of them.

I noticed when we arrived that they had left two spare seats for us. Lauren sat next to one of the spare seats. Octavian sat next to her, but he hardly got to talk with her because Georgina, as usual, dominated the conversation.

Georgina was choosing to have us close. That got me to thinking. If she was guilty, there would be no reason to latch on to a pair of strangers just before committing the murder and keep them along ever since. No, she must be innocent, but she had to know that someone in her group did it. Georgina was many things, but I could tell she wasn't dumb.

So, what was her motivation to have us here? Was she afraid she might be next and hoped having witnesses around might protect her? Did she see Maggie's murder coming and grab us into their circle right at the beginning in the hope that the murderer would get scared and not go through with it?

It was time to put our plan into action.

Octavian leaned in and whispered something in Lauren's ear. The rest of the table leaned in, trying to catch it. It was like a strong wind had come and blown us all over.

Lauren laughed at whatever Octavian had said and gave me a sly look.

Once when I was in El Salvador, I stayed at a particularly nasty hotel. It was part of an undercover operation where I was posing as a drug addict. That hotel sure fit the role. I came out of my room one night, pretending I was going to try and score on the street as a way to sniff out the local dealers, when I saw a man from another room come out at the same time I did. The walls were so thin he probably heard me get up, put on my shoes, and get ready to leave, and he timed it so he could come out at the same moment, as if by coincidence. He gave me that exact same sly look.

To my surprise, he didn't attack, which told me what I wanted to know. I went around the corner of the hallway, counted to ten, and went back.

He had already jimmied the lock on my door, entered my room, and drawn a knife, obviously so that he could grab me when I came back.

I broke his nose, his collarbone, three ribs, and hopefully changed his assumptions about the likely victimhood of lone foreign women staying at shoddy hotels.

Breaking Lauren's collarbone sounded like fun. It probably wouldn't advance the case, though, and if I tried to break someone's bones these days, I'd just as likely break one of my own in the process.

Lauren whispered something back to Octavian, and soon they were in a secret conclave. I pretended to be oblivious. I'm good at feigning stupidity when I need to. Getting your enemy to underestimate you is an age-old tactic. It was impossible to hear what they were saying anyway. The dining room was a lot more raucous now that we were sharing the cruise with young people.

In the meantime, I got into a conversation with

Fiona, who sat to my other side. Other than Georgina, she took the most care in her appearance and was constantly looking into a compact mirror to make sure her (overly caked on) makeup was looking right. As we talked, she added an extra bit of powder to hide her drinker's nose.

"I think I'm going to sue the DMV," I said with a chuckle. "I renewed my license last year, and they did a horrid job with my photo. It's just so embarrassing."

I pulled out my driver's license and showed her. It was, indeed, a bad photo.

"Oh, it's not so bad," Fiona said in a tone that showed she thought the opposite. "The problem is that they're so lazy there. I suppose it comes from having to process so many people and the fact that they only hire subnormals. You have to be assertive with that sort. Get yourself dolled up and looking your best, and make sure to adjust the lights yourself and clean the lens of the camera. They're always so filthy. Look at mine. It came out all right."

She pulled out her license. I murmured something nice about her picture and took note of her last name. Fiona Harrison. Bingo. That was all I needed. I could track her down and, through her, find the others and hopefully dig up something useful. I got her address too.

By now everyone had gotten into some serious drinking. Their morning hangovers had long since been forgotten, thanks to the Bloody Marys, and now they were drinking piña coladas and shrieking hysterically over some juicy bit of gossip about someone back in Schenectady. The food arrived, which prompted someone to order another round. I was beginning to feel a bit woozy. I used to be able to hold my own in a drinking competition, but by age seventy-one, I was well out of practice and did not have the iron liver this gang of harpies obviously did.

I tried and failed to get the conversation around to Maggie.

"Who wants to talk about that old loser?" Fiona sputtered, dribbling some of her drink on the tablecloth.

So instead of furthering the case, I had to endure lots of shallow conversation about nothing in particular. It certainly reinforced my perception of them.

"Oh, hey!" Octavian said to the table. Besides Georgina, he was the only one who the entire group would stop what they were saying and listen to. "I just remembered. Tony Iron and the Bar Belles are going to be playing in the disco in an hour. What do you say we get changed into our best duds and go dance the night away?"

They all thought it was a brilliant idea, especially Lauren, who sidled up to him. We finished our meal and went as a group back to our cabins, passing crowds of buoyant young gay men and rather subdued (one might say intimidated) senior citizens. Georgina and the rest of them sneered.

"Why did they have to put them on *our* ship?" Brenda grumbled.

"They had engine trouble," Octavian replied. "I suppose there wasn't much choice."

"They should have left them drifting in the sea," Brenda said. The others nodded.

That was the first time I had heard Brenda give an opinion on anything. I hoped it would be the last.

We went back to our respective cabins, Octavian stopping Lauren from coming into his, and got ready for the concert. I took the opportunity to drink a tall glass of water. It was a good way to stave off or at least reduce the hangover that was sure to come. If I didn't moderate my drinking around these people, the next corpse might be mine.

I got into a nice blue dress I had bought especially for the cruise and waited for a few minutes. I wanted Octavian to work his magic before I went back into the hallway. He was playing his part admirably. When I did come out of my cabin, I saw Octavian had changed into a tailored suit that made him look ten years younger. The other "ladies" in our group had noticed, too, and were fawning over him.

I decided I had spent too much time playing the clueless dupe, and I needed to ramp up the tension.

"Octavian!" I scolded in my best shrewish-old-lady voice. "It's like I've turned into the invisible woman."

I shouldered my way through the crowd and hooked my arm into his, and we walked down the hall, followed by the poorly stifled snickers of the others.

Octavian looked abashed. I think that was more than playacting. I think he really did feel guilty. What a darling. He wouldn't have survived five minutes in the CIA.

I think we were all surprised to find the disco packed, and not just by senior citizens who remembered Tony Iron and the Bar Belles from their youth but by a large crowd of gay men. Why these people would care about a band old enough to be their grandparents and whose last hit had come out before most of them were born was beyond me.

But there they were, eagerly anticipating the

curtain coming up. As we passed through the crowd, I eavesdropped.

"The best song is 'Powerlifting Love.' I work out to that all the time."

"My favorite is 'Bench Press Baby.'"

"Oh, come on. That's dedicated to a *girl*!"

"No, it isn't. You have to read between the lines."

"He probably wrote it for a girl just to make the public happy. But we know what he's *really* talking about."

I shook my head. Tony Iron and the Bar Belles had become some sort of gay icon? Why? I suppose back when he was young, he might have caught the eye of some gay men, but he always sang about women and surrounded himself with women. If they were going to pick an old star to follow, wouldn't they rather latch onto Liberace or Elton John?

We found a place on the dance floor just in time for the curtain to come up. The polite applause from the senior citizens was drowned out by a roar from the gay men. Tony Iron and the Bar Belles were already in position, probably to spare them the embarrassment of having to hobble onstage in front of their fans.

Tony Iron flexed his arms, which were still impressively muscled for someone who had to be well into his eighties, and shouted into the microphone, "Who's ready to sweat?"

"We are!" we shouted back. Tony Iron always started his concerts that way.

"Want to do some fly curls with me?" he shouted.

"Yes!"

He wiggled his eyebrows, still mysteriously black after all these years. "And how about some leg lifts?"

"Yes!"

"Oh, yeah, baby!" a man who couldn't have been older than twenty-five shouted nearby, bouncing up and down.

I stared at him. What was going on?

Tony Iron shaded his eyes and looked around in mock surprise. "There seem to be a lot more passengers on board than when we left port."

This brought some laughter and cheers.

Then in that soft, silky voice that had made him famous, Tony Iron asked, "You boys ready to party?"

The gay half of the crowd went wild while the old half looked around in confusion.

"Then let's party!" he shouted and launched into "I'll Be Your Stair Master."

It was one of his biggest and raciest hits, about "climbing the staircase of your love to be your master." All about a man sweeping a woman off her feet and her being helpless (and unwilling) to resist.

At least that's what I thought it was about.

When five hugely muscular men, all clad in leather, leapt on stage and began strutting around, lines like "I'll whip you into shape. I'll crush you like a grape. I'll be your stair maaaaster!" took on a whole new meaning.

I glanced at Octavian.

He was staring at his workout guru with utter disbelief. "No ..." I saw his mouth form the word but couldn't hear over the guitar solo. "Tony Iron couldn't be ..."

"Queer as a three-dollar bill, baby!" a young man beside us cheered.

Octavian turned to him. "Seriously?"

"Seriously," the youth replied with a grin. "Why do you think a guy that popular never got married? And now that he can, he's too old. Civil rights came too late for him."

"But not for us," said another young man, literally sweeping the first man off his feet.

Octavian looked back at Tony Iron, cocked his head, squinted, thought for a moment, and shrugged. "Want to dance?" he asked me.

"All right."

I felt happy to get some attention from him again, although I wasn't quite sure how to dance to "I'll Be Your Stair Master." It wasn't a slow dance, and I sure wasn't going to dance the way those young men in the crowd were dancing, even if I still could.

I took Octavian by the hands and moved in close. He laughed and stepped back.

"Don't you remember the Stair Master dance?" He turned to face the stage, had me do the same, and started moving his legs up and down like he was climbing stairs in time to the music.

"Oh, I remember that!" some octogenarian shouted and started doing the same.

"What's that?" the young man who had been talking to Octavian asked.

"The Stair Master dance," Octavian replied. "This was big when your parents were still courting."

The man and his partner started doing the same, lifting their legs much higher than Octavian or I could manage.

Soon more and more fans, both old and young, started doing the Stair Master, knees rising high, arms pumping as we sang along with Tony Iron, "I want to be your stair maaaster!"

I glanced around, legs still pumping, glad I couldn't hear my knees pop, and was amazed. The dance rippled out across the packed dance floor like a wave on a pond after a stone was thrown into it. Octavian had gotten the whole crowd doing the dance. Tony Iron flashed a thumbs-up from the stage. The Bar Belles beamed at us, eyes sparkling.

Lauren cut in front of me, Stair Mastering her way over to Octavian. He danced with her for a minute, flashed me a conspiratorial look, and danced over to Fiona, who blushed and bopped like a schoolgirl, basking in the attention.

Lauren, who was behind Octavian now, gave Fiona a nod of approval.

Wait. Lauren didn't care that Octavian was choosing Fiona over her. Ah! The point wasn't who got Octavian, the point was to take Octavian away from me. It wasn't about their happiness. It was about my misery.

What a vile little crew we had landed ourselves among.

And Octavian had sussed it out. Clever man. Maybe he could have done well in the CIA after all.

I kept Stair Mastering, pretending to be so starstruck by what was happening on stage that I didn't notice my boyfriend flirting with all and sundry.

The song reached its crescendo, the sound of a

thousand feet stomping in time to the beat, when all of a sudden, there was a disturbance to my left. There was a feminine scream and a wave of people moving out of the way.

Alicia fell to the floor, smacking face-first into the smooth wood. She twitched a few times and then lay still. Blood began to spread from her body.

NINE

Nothing kills a fun evening quicker than a murder on the dance floor. Worried whispers and cries of fear spread through the crowd as fast as Octavian's dance had done a few minutes previously. One by one, the Bar Belles stopped playing their instruments. Tony Iron, who was singing with his eyes closed, kept on going until the lead guitarist poked him in the back with her instrument.

"I'll be your stair maaaa—hey, what's going on?"

"She's been murdered!" I shouted. "No one touch the body. No one leaves this room!" I shouted.

More gasps followed by a profound silence.

A young man pushed his way through the crowd. When I say young, he looked in his thirties, which made him notably older than the average in the gay crowd.

"I'm a doctor. Stand aside," he said. He knelt by her, felt her pulse, and turned her over. Alicia's nose was broken. A pool of blood glistened where she had smacked her face into the floor.

"You shouldn't—" I started.

"Quiet," he cut me off. He put an ear to her chest. "Get me the defibrillator!"

A waiter rushed up with the device, and the doctor applied it to Alicia's chest. There was a loud *thunk*, and Alicia's body convulsed. He listened to her chest again. I glanced at Georgina and her pals. They were all pale, obviously shocked. But who was faking? How had they killed her? And why?

The doctor applied the defibrillator again. Alicia convulsed again and groaned. The doctor felt her pulse, timing it with his watch. Then he nodded.

"The worst is over, but we need to get her to the infirmary."

"What happened?" Georgina asked.

"She suffered cardiac arrest. Too much dancing and drinking for a woman her age," the doctor replied.

"Are you sure?" I asked. Maybe she had been poisoned or something.

The doctor gave me a warning look. "You can't party like you're in your twenties anymore."

Two sailors rushed through the crowd, carrying a stretcher. They put Alicia on it and hurried off, the doctor, me, and Georgina and her crew following.

"You're going to be all right, Alicia," Georgina choked out, walking alongside the stretcher, tears in her eyes. Alicia moaned, barely conscious.

We got to the infirmary, where we were met by the ship's doctor and a nurse, who had already been alerted. They briefly consulted with the doctor who had revived Alicia then took her inside, closing the door on the rest of us.

It was then that I noticed Octavian and Fiona weren't with us.

I felt a spike of jealousy, a wholly unworthy emotion since I knew Octavian was "on the case," as it were. I hoped that was the only thing he was on.

For a moment, everyone stood there in silence. Georgina started pacing, giving me odd looks. Lauren burst into tears and excused herself.

"I can't stand it. I just can't stand it!" she cried as she hurried off.

Finally, a real emotion from one of these succubi.

Lauren came back a few minutes later, her mascara still a mess. She must have been really upset not to freshen up, as obsessive as she was about her appearance. Appearances were the only thing this group cared about.

After an agonizing wait, the ship's doctor opened the door.

Georgina rushed up to him. "Is she all right?"

The doctor nodded. "Your friend is in stable condition. We've called a medevac. The helicopter will be here in an hour to take her to a hospital on the islands."

"Can we see her?" Brenda asked.

"In a little bit, once she's rested." He closed the door on us again.

After a few minutes, the gay doctor from the disco came out.

"Where are you going, buster?" Georgina demanded. "My friend needs you in there."

"The ship's doctor can take over from here. He's got a full clinic and has two nurses on duty. Don't worry. Your friend is going to be just fine. She needs rest more than anything."

Georgina's face grew red. "So, what now? You're just going to go back to the disco and booze the night away while my friend is dying in the infirmary?"

"She's not dying," he replied in a calm voice.

"But she will if she keeps up all this drinking and partying."

He turned and left.

"My God, how irresponsible!" Georgina shouted. "Come on, girls. Let's get a drink while we're waiting."

We retired to the nearest bar. On this ship there was always a bar nearby. No doubt the designers had planned it that way.

The bar was quiet, most people still being at the disco. My companions each ordered a stiff one. I ordered a coffee. I had a feeling it was going to be a long night.

No one spoke much. For once Georgina was silent, pensive. The rest of her crowd, lacking her lead, couldn't think of anything to say. I had the impression that if it had been Georgina who had been thrown off the ship or suffered a heart attack, they would have immediately gone in search of a new leader just so they would have some kind of identity for themselves.

After she had knocked back her drink, Georgina turned to Charlotte, Brenda, and Lauren.

"Girls, go find Fiona. She needs to know what happened."

All three got up. I found it odd that she wanted

to send all of them when only one needed to go. They obeyed without hesitation, like they always did.

"We'll look in the disco," Charlotte said.

"And the cabins," Lauren said under her breath but loud enough for me to hear. The others snickered.

Georgina turned to me, trying to control a smug smile. After a moment she grew serious.

"Why did you think someone had tried to murder Alicia?"

I shifted in my seat, unsure what to say. While I didn't think Georgina was the killer, I couldn't know that for sure.

It turned out I didn't need to answer, because Georgina answered for me.

She glanced over her shoulder, leaned forward, and said in a low voice, "You were wrong about Alicia. Her doctor warned her of her heart condition. Fiona takes her vital signs every day. Didn't you notice Alicia always drinks less than the rest of us?"

No, I hadn't noticed. There had been so many drinks and so many rounds and so many quick nips in their cabins that I couldn't keep track.

Georgina glanced over her shoulder again and whispered so softly that I could barely hear her. "No one tried to murder her, but somebody murdered Maggie."

I didn't have to feign my look of surprise. Here she was actually admitting one of her friends was a murderer!

"Who?" I asked. "And why?"

Georgina rubbed her temples, suddenly looking old and tired.

"I don't know who. It could have been any of them. And why? Because Maggie was dangerous."

"Dangerous how?"

"Back home she's been spreading nasty rumors about us. Saying all sorts of horrible things like we were man stealers and that we tried to undercut other people's relationships and happiness."

"No. I couldn't imagine you doing such a horrible thing."

"And she claimed that we had been having dalliances with certain married men. Prominent ones too."

"Impossible!"

"I know," she sniffed. "After all we did for her, she turns on us like this and spreads malicious lies."

"But why?"

"Because of the bowling tournament. I told you. She couldn't get over being rejected for the team."

Hmmm, it looked like there was only so much truth I was going to get out of this witness. It was a pity she was a civilian and not some drug lord or terrorist. I could have brought in a CIA interrogation squad that would have gotten her talking even before they finished unpacking their toolkit. Most of the time, just seeing the toolkit was enough.

We only did that on bad people. Really bad people. Not even Georgina was bad enough to qualify.

"But why kill her?"

"When she saw us on deck, she got paranoid. She thought we were after her. She bumped into us in the hallway shortly thereafter while you and Octavian were still on deck. She threatened us. Claimed she had information that would make it so that we could never show our faces in Schenectady again."

"What sort of information?"

Georgina made a dismissive wave with her hand. "Nothing. She had cooked up some sort of conspiracy theory about us going around systematically destroying marriages. She was crazy. But one of the girls must have gotten scared. What are we without our reputations? And it wasn't like anyone would miss Maggie. She was a loser, but she wasn't suicidal. She was too determined to prove herself to quit it all. I think one of them pushed her off the ship."

"But who?"

Georgina ordered another drink. "I don't know. Lord help me, but I don't know."

I'm not an overly religious person, but when someone like her calls on the Lord, it makes me a bit queasy. That drug baron I went to El Salvador to catch wore a big gold cross and donated to his local church while at the same time burying his victims in a mass grave in the jungle outside of town. You can have faith and live a religious life, or you can be evil. You can't be both. I wish more people understood that. The world would be a better place.

"So why are you telling me all this?"

She grabbed me by the shoulders. Her grip was surprisingly strong.

"Because I need you. You're a smart woman, Barbara. I could see right from the start that you suspected Maggie had been pushed. You've been asking probing questions and studying us. If anyone can help me, it's you. I can't go to the police, because I have no evidence, just a hunch. I need you to help me find who killed her. I'm afraid she might kill again. Do you know that when Alicia fell down, for a moment, I thought someone had poisoned her drink?

I think someone in our group is so desperate to keep the status quo that they've gone crazy and will kill anyone who gets in the way. But you can help find out who it is. You're objective. I'm so close to these people I can't think straight, but you can look at everyone with an outsider's eye. Will you help? Please say you will."

Before I could reply, the rest of the gang showed up, Octavian and Fiona included.

"They say we can see Alicia now," Brenda told us. "Alicia asked to speak to Georgina alone first."

Everyone started filing out of the bar. Octavian gave me a look that said he had something important to tell me. I gave him a tiny nod and followed the crowd.

Georgina moved in close beside me and spoke to me in a low voice, "I'll see Alicia first but not alone. You need to be there. I have a feeling she has something to say that you need to hear."

TEN

As we entered the infirmary, we passed a room where another senior citizen lay groaning. The sharp smell of disinfectant couldn't quite hide the stench of vomit coming from in there. It looked like Alicia wasn't the only person who needed to realize her party days were over.

Alicia lay very still and pale in her bed. She was hooked up to a heart monitor, which showed a weak and irregular pulse. I'm hardly an expert, but that jagged line sure didn't look healthy. Cotton gauze was stuck in both her nostrils, and her nose was twisted at a bad angle. The doctor stood beside Alicia's bed, talking to her.

"Now, Ms. Ponsette, I just got an email from your hospital back home. You had been warned about your heart condition and told to avoid alcohol and not to exert yourself. You're very lucky there was a doctor on the dance floor. Otherwise we might not be having this conversation."

"A doctor on the dance floor?" Her voice sounded weak.

"Yes, another passenger. Good thing for you that other boat had engine trouble."

Alicia's eyes widened. "One of the gay ones?"

The doctor looked confused. "I fail to see why that matters, Ms. Ponsette."

Alicia's face took on an expression of horror. The heart monitor showed a faster and more jagged pulse. "Did he ... touch me? He didn't do mouth-to-mouth resuscitation, did he? You need to give me a blood test!"

"He saved your life, Ms. Ponsette," the doctor said sharply. Then he turned to us. "You can only have a minute. Try to keep her calm."

With that, the doctor went to see to his other patient.

We drew closer to the bed.

"How are you feeling?" Georgina asked, stroking her hair with what looked like genuine affection.

"Violated," Alicia groaned. "I can't believe he touched me."

"Perhaps he shouldn't have," I said. I didn't mean to say that. It just sort of slipped out.

"He should have waited for the ship's doctor to come or let Fiona treat me, but doctors always lord it over nurses, don't they?" Alicia said. "But let's not talk about that now. I need to tell you something, Georgina."

Alicia glanced at me, expecting me to leave.

"Barbara is here to help," Georgina said. "You can say anything in front of her."

After a moment's hesitation, she said softly, "It's about Maggie. Somebody killed her."

"How do you know that?" Georgina asked, surprised.

"When I went back to my cabin that night, I found my bowling ball covered in blood."

Georgina gasped.

Alicia went on. "That's why I said I forgot it. I couldn't bring it to the bowling alley, and I was afraid to clean it, to even touch it. Someone got into my cabin and used my bowling ball to knock Maggie over her head and then dump her in the sea. They used my bowling ball to shift the blame on someone else. I didn't do it, though. I swear. Otherwise I would have cleaned the ball, and no one would have been any the wiser. The key card to my cabin is in my purse. Take it, and go get my ball. Go to the ship's security, and tell them everything."

"But, Alicia, why didn't you tell anyone before?" I asked.

"I was afraid. Oh, I was so afraid. When I saw blood on my bowling ball, I fell faint. Good thing I fell on the bed. My heart was in palpitations for several minutes, and I was hyperventilating. I hid the bowling ball in the closet and had Fiona check on me. She made me take a hot shower to soothe my nerves and rest for a couple of hours. I knew I shouldn't have gone out tonight, but I didn't want to disappoint you, Georgina. We all came to have fun together."

"Yes, but this was a murder. Why didn't you report it?" I insisted.

"Because the murderer was trying to stick it on me, don't you see?" she cried, raising her voice. The heart monitor started gyrating wildly. We soothed her, and she took several deep breaths. After a minute the monitor went back to showing a regular heartbeat. "I figured if I stayed silent, it would all blow over. Maggie was already dead, after all, and nobody would miss her, but then this heart attack made me think twice. We were horrid to her, Georgina, like we've been horrid to a lot of people.

Something like this was bound to happen eventually."

Georgina's lip curled in disgust, and she stepped away.

"Who did you share your cabin with?" I asked.

"No one. With my condition, it's better for me to stay alone. I get less antsy that way. I have no idea how they got into my cabin."

I studied her. Could she be the murderer and just be covering up? Unlikely, with that heart condition. A stressful incident like murdering someone in cold blood would have probably knocked her down. Plus, she was about to be evacuated and get away from the scene of the crime. If she was guilty, she would have no reason to confess all this and tell us the murder weapon was in a cabin only she could access.

Georgina got the key card from Alicia's purse. There was a knock on the door, and the others came in. The two of us said goodbye and left.

We made a beeline for Alicia's cabin.

Georgina unlocked the cabin door, and we entered, flicking on the light. It looked almost identical to my own cabin except that the closet was stuffed with colorful dresses and the bathroom counter was covered in medicine bottles. Why a woman with that many prescriptions thought she could drink and dance all night was beyond me. She really risked her life just to please Georgina?

Georgina rummaged around the closet. After my quick survey, I helped. We didn't find the bowling ball in the closet or anywhere else.

"Gone," Georgina said.

"Or it never existed."

"She had her own ball. We all did."

I remembered seeing the other balls in the bowling alley. They all had their names and the logo of their team. Alicia would be sure to have one.

"Then where is it?" I asked.

Georgina shrugged.

"Did she give an extra key to anyone else?" I asked.

"Not that I know of. I know Fiona didn't have one because this evening, when she went to take Alicia's vital signs, I saw her knock on the door to be let in. I wasn't given an extra key to my room anyway. Were you?"

"No."

We stood there for a moment, stumped.

"The cleaning lady could have taken it," Georgina said, sounding a bit unsure of herself.

"Who steals a bowling ball?"

Georgina inclined her head. "True. Alicia must have lent her key to someone."

"She would have mentioned that because that would be the obvious culprit."

Georgina threw her hands in the air. "Then it's impossible! How could the ball be gone?"

"Wait." I pulled my key card out. It was a simple electronic card that came in a little paper folder with my room number on it. I put it beside Alicia's room card. They were identical. Like in hotels, the front desk activated one when a guest checked in and deactivated it when they checked out. The only way to tell the difference between them was the paper folder with the room number written on it.

Georgina took in a sharp breath. "Someone switched the cards while we were all out then snuck back here, took the ball, and then switched the cards back again."

I nodded. Georgina was smart. Perhaps "cunning" was the better word.

"When could that have happened?" I asked.

Georgina shrugged. "Any time. We were all sticking together, and we've been out and about ever since the ship launched."

"It couldn't have been any time," I said as we walked out of the room and closed the door behind us. "Let's try to narrow it down. It had to be a time when Alicia was present and you were all distracted enough by some activity that the murderer could have switched the cards then excused herself for a minute. And it had to have been after Maggie was killed and before you all went bowling because Alicia didn't bring the ball."

By silent agreement, we headed on deck. The others would be coming back to our hall soon, and we did not want to meet up with them yet.

Georgina considered for a moment. "Let's see ... we were at the bar late the night Maggie was killed. Then we hung out in the cabins for a bit. Then breakfast, lunch, the bar, dinner, the bar ... oh, it just goes on and on! We all sat together, and our purses were lying within easy reach. And the girls were always excusing themselves to go freshen up."

This was a problem. It wasn't surprising that Georgina couldn't come up with anything. Most people are terrible witnesses. They don't pay attention until after they know a crime has been committed. Why would they? Georgina could hardly be expected to watch her friends with an eagle eye when she didn't even know one would try and switch the key cards. And she couldn't be expected to remember each and every time someone left to ostensibly go to the bathroom.

"So who do you think might have wanted to kill Maggie?"

Georgina shook her head and sighed. We had made it to an observation platform on one of the lower decks. There was a floor-to-ceiling Plexiglas window. We stood looking out to sea.

"I don't know. I just don't know. I never thought one of us could do such a thing, and then to try and blame it on Alicia? Why? We all get along so well."

I turned to Georgina and looked her in the eye.

"You need to be straight with me," I said.

She didn't reply, her eyes looking in every direction except at mine.

I went on. "Georgina, you brought us into your circle the moment you met us. Perhaps you do that a lot, but even after the blowup with Maggie and her saying all those nasty things about you to us, you kept us close. And you continued to keep us close even after Maggie went into the sea. You've suspected that she was killed all along, haven't you? You probably expected someone to bump her off even before it happened."

Georgina bit her lip and trembled. It was shocking to see such a normally confident (well, arrogant) woman suddenly so afraid. I have to admit, it gave me a sense of smug satisfaction.

"I ... the thought crossed my mind."

"Why?"

"She was so vindictive, trying to undercut our reputations that way. Everyone in the group said she needed to be shut up. They were quite nasty about it. I tried to calm them down, but they really wanted to drive her out of town. When she bumped into us on deck and started badmouthing us to you and Octavian, two complete strangers, I got a sinking feeling that one of the girls would try something."

"Did any one of them show more hatred than the rest? Did Maggie hurt one more than the others?"

She shook her head and wiped a tear from her eye. At least she made the motion. She did it so quickly I didn't see the actual tear. "I have no idea which one of them did it. It's all so horrible."

"Did you know Maggie would be on this cruise?"

She shrugged. "We planned it months ago, when we were still trying to make something of her. We invited her along, but after we stopped speaking with one another, we assumed she wouldn't go on this cruise. I guess she assumed the same about us."

"So why did she have a falling out with you?"

"The bowling tournament. I told you."

"Nothing else?"

She shrugged again. "She was hypersensitive. I know it's such a petty thing to get angry about, but that's how she was."

Liar. Georgina wasn't going to tell me about Wesley.

I decided to try another tactic.

"You know, maybe we have it all wrong. Maybe she really did jump, and Alicia was having a hallucination about the bowling ball. Alicia just survived cardiac arrest. She isn't thinking straight. Is there any reason why Maggie might want to kill herself? Did she have any major trauma recently?"

For a second the mask slipped. Georgina gave me a cold, calculating look, obviously wondering how much I had discovered. Then she once again became the distraught, kindly woman who needed a friend. "Not that I know of. Her life has been one long series of disappointments. I think that final rejection by us might have snapped her sanity. I don't think she killed herself, though. It just wasn't in her nature, and what about the missing bowling ball?"

"That's right. You're very intelligent, Georgina."

She beamed despite acting distraught a moment before. Nothing gets to the heart of an arrogant person more than flattery. Her group of followers had certainly figured that out.

"I'm afraid, Barbara. I think my friends have become overly attached to me. I love them all dearly, but they follow me around like hens. Surely you've noticed. I'm tired of having to be the mother hen. They look to me for everything. You know I had to plan this entire trip? It's exhausting. They've become obsessed with me. They call me all the time, ask me for advice about every little thing. And when Maggie started saying bad things about me around the neighborhood, they were enraged. I tremble to say this, Barbara, but I think one of them murdered Maggie for my sake."

I considered this. She certainly did have them in thrall. These were insecure women getting their sense of identity from a stronger personality. If that personality were threatened, it could lead one or more of them to kill. I'd seen it before in cults and extremist groups. People could even be motivated to kill themselves.

But how to find out who did it? Alicia didn't have the heart, literally, and she had just made that confession about the ball. Charlotte, Brenda, Fiona, and Lauren were all equally invested in the group, and all equally likely suspects. Lauren was the youngest by a few years and perhaps the strongest, but all of them were remarkably strong thanks to their bowling. I had never realized it was such a workout. Maybe the Marine Corps should use it in boot camp.

What else did I know? Both Lauren and Fiona had tried to poach my boyfriend and didn't seem to mind the competition from each other. That seemed like a group game, so that didn't get me anywhere. Charlotte suffered from malaria, at least that's what she said, and that could weaken a person. Perhaps she didn't have the strength to kill Maggie, but I couldn't know that for sure.

So what else did I know about these people? Practically nothing. They hardly ever spoke an original thought, merely following Georgina's lead.

But wait, what was it that Lauren said when she was giving us bowling tips?

That Maggie wasn't as bad of a bowler as Georgina had said. That was the only time I had heard one of them contradict Georgina.

She had said something else too: "She sure was competition in other matters."

She had said this on the sly, like a child badmouthing a teacher or strict parent behind their back. She had been about to go on when that gay couple had walked in.

I needed to find out what she was going to say.

Unfortunately, in my role as the jealous girl-friend trying to keep her from Octavian, I couldn't have a private chat with her without her being on her guard.

I'd have to get Octavian to do it.

Poor man. I'm sure this wasn't what he was thinking when he invited me on a cruise.

ELEVEN

It turned out Octavian had exceeded my expectations. He showed up at my cabin shortly after I got back.

"So, what happened with you and Fiona?" I asked after I let him in, checking that no one else was in the hallway and saw him enter.

Octavian reddened. "She's just as bad as Lauren. She's just as bad as all of them. Why in the world did these Gorgons decide to befriend us if all they wanted to do was split us apart?"

"Because we were convenient targets and looked happy. If we hadn't been in this wing, they would have found a different set of victims."

"Well, we're not going to be victims," he said with a frown. "We're going to hunt down whoever murdered that poor woman and have her brought to justice. That should break up their little coven."

"My my, you're acting like quite the crusader."

"They insulted me, Barbara, thinking their very dubious charms could pull me away from you. And they insulted you by trying."

"So, um, what happened?"

Octavian stood a little straighter. "Nothing happened. I'm not that kind of guy."

I laughed. "You're adorable. No, I mean what did she say?"

"Oh, well that's where it gets interesting. Besides trying to take you from me, she started giving me all sorts of dirt on Brenda. That surprised me. I figured she'd try to undercut Lauren since Lauren had made a play for me before Fiona did. But it's a game for them, as you say. It's not about getting me; it's about hurting us. Well, there's a rivalry between Fiona and Brenda. That sure isn't any game."

"What kind of rivalry?" I asked, taking two cans of tomato juice out of the minibar. We both could use it after all the booze we'd been guzzling with our new fake friends.

"A petty one, of course, but nasty all the same. Fiona and Brenda each claim to have come up with the name for their bowling team. I gather it was one of the few times one of Georgina's followers came up with an idea that Georgina really liked."

"And whoever did would be second hen in the pecking order."

"She would indeed, but the problem is both make the claim, and nobody else in the group is coming down on one side or the other."

"Not even Georgina?"

"Nope. Turns out one of them came up with the name while they were all having a late-night boozer, and everyone was too drunk to remember whose idea it was."

"Maybe Fiona and Brenda don't remember either."

"That's entirely likely. They've dug in, though, and each is trying to convince everyone else. Lauren told me the rest of them are sick of it and worry it's going to tear the group apart. That's why they're all staying neutral."

"Too bad. That group deserves to be torn apart."

"I also had a little powwow with Lauren and learned what she was going to tell us at the bowling alley."

"I was just about to ask you to try and find that out."

"Great minds think alike, pretty lady. It turns out that Maggie fell for some guy named Wesley."

"He showed up on her Facebook feed."

"Did he? I'm not surprised. He was the one love of her life. They met in the library, where he was researching a book on moles."

"Moles? As in the animal?"

"No, as in the skin blemish. He was finding examples of moles that looked like things. Texas, the first Apple computer, the starship *Enterprise*, the Teapot Dome Scandal ..."

"How can a mole look like the Teapot Dome Scandal?"

"Do I look like a mole expert? I guess we'll have to wait until the book comes out. It's going to be a coffee table book. A conversation starter to break the ice at parties. He's already got a publisher. Anyway, he was researching this in her library and noticed she had a mole that looked like Michelangelo's David. He asked to photograph it, and love bloomed."

"These two people sound terribly desperate."

"I don't judge. At least they aren't psychic vampires like our cruise companions."

"True enough. But don't ask to photograph my moles. I'm too old for that sort of thing."

He leaned forward, squinting at my shoulder.

"You know ..." He pointed at one of my moles. "That looks an awful lot like an '82 Nissan Stanza."

"Go on with your story before I slap you."

Octavian sighed. "No sense of humor. So it wasn't long before Maggie was showing off her new beau all around town. They were sloppy in love, holding hands in the park, sharing the same milkshake, even waltzing in the street."

"Waltzing in the street?"

"They got arrested for it. Got a fine for blocking traffic."

"Remind me never to go to Schenectady."

"Why? Do you like to waltz in the street?" He took my hands and got them into position.

"Do go on. We have a murder to solve."

He waltzed me around the cabin. "It turns out that Wesley was famous, or perhaps infamous, around Schenectady for seeing all sorts of strange things in people's moles. People either loved him or hated him, thought he was a harmless loon or some strange variety of pervert. I'm undecided myself. Well, Georgina decided she wanted to be in the book and thought she had a mole on her thigh that looked like Excalibur stuck in the stone. She went to Wesley and raised her skirt to show off this dermatological wonder, and Wesley told her that her mole looked like a frog catching a fly with its tongue and that he didn't want to photograph her mole because he had already found an editor of a UFO magazine in Cleveland who had a mole that looked much more like a frog catching a fly."

"UFOs were bound to come into this eventually," I said, admiring Octavian's ability as a dancer. "Georgina is just petty enough to be offended by losing out to a UFOlogist."

"She was more than offended. She was apoplectic with rage. Maggie was getting in the book, and she wasn't, and that just wouldn't do. So she decided to drive a wedge between them."

I stopped in my tracks. Suddenly I didn't feel like dancing anymore.

"Wesley looks positively sane by comparison," I said.

Octavian met my eye. "It gets worse. Brenda tried to woo him away from Maggie, but that didn't work. Fiona tried too. No dice. Wesley was too devoted to his new girlfriend to be wooed."

I gave him a peck on the cheek. "Just like you. You're unwooable."

"Don't compare me to Wesley. I don't collect moles."

"You have the honor of a Wesley and the class of an Octavian."

"That's better. So once they realized they couldn't break up that relationship like they usually did, they got nasty."

"They weren't nasty before?"

"You ain't seen nothing yet. They had Alicia go to see Wesley, claiming she had an interesting mole, and then she claimed he made unwanted advances on her."

"No!"

"She even tried to press charges, but Wesley's attorney brought in dozens of character witnesses showing how awful these people were, and the case was dropped."

"Georgina is concerned about her reputation in Schenectady. It looks like she doesn't realize her reputation is already terrible."

"That woman is a few plates short of a picnic. But anyway, Wesley was so crushed by the accusations, and by the whisperfest that surrounded the whole affair, that he left Schenectady, never to return."

"And so they got their way and ruined Wesley's and Maggie's love. I'm surprised one of them killed Maggie and not the other way around. But I'm curious about one thing. Why would Lauren tell you all this?"

"I don't know. Do you think it's all lies? Or is Lauren playing some sort of game?"

"We're going to find out."

"I'll question her," Octavian said, moving to the door.

"Oh no, let me do it. I don't want you to get falsely accused of anything. Besides, I have a little trick up my sleeve that I think will get Lauren to spill the truth."

I sent Octavian back to his cabin and brewed up a plan.

It was time for a showdown.

While I had never been on a cruise before, I had been to many fine hotels, and I'd learned a few things about how they operated. One of them was that the staff were overworked, underpaid, and generally willing to take bribes if you asked them the right way. Guests at big hotels were always asking for something "extra," often illegal or at least immoral. And a cruise ship was basically a big hotel on water.

So I rang the service bell and within five minutes had a young man named Phil standing at my door. He looked fresh out of college.

"Hello, Phil, are you fresh out of college?"

"Why yes I am, ma'am."

Isn't it nice to have your perceptions confirmed?

"What did you major in?"

"Electrical engineering, ma'am."

"Times are tough, Phil. You have a useful degree that should get you a fine job, and here you are serving drinks."

Phil stiffened. "Oh, I'm very happy with my job, ma'am."

"No, you're not, Phil. You deserve more. Would you like this?" I held out a hundred dollars.

He stepped back. "I don't give massages to passengers."

I blinked. That was not the reaction I had expected. After a moment, I realized I was a bit more innocent than I thought I was. Poor little Phil was quite handsome. He probably got offers like this from passengers all the time.

"No, Phil. I don't want a massage. What I want is for you to do a little something for me ..."

TWELVE

"Ready? One, two, three!"

We knocked back our drinks. Lauren and I sat in my cabin, having our third round of piña coladas.

Well, Lauren was having her third round of extra-strong piña coladas, while I was having my third virgin piña colada. Phil was serving them as fast as we could drink them, with special instructions to make sure the bartender brewed one strong one and one safe one and to make sure I got the safe one.

I had gone to her door, pounded on it, and raged at her for trying to steal Octavian, who had made himself scarce on my instructions. I then told her that Octavian only liked strong women, and a weakling like her would never get his heart. She had snapped back that she could do anything I could do, only ten times better.

So I challenged her to a drinking contest, saying that if I won, she would lay off, and if she won, I would step aside. Drinking was such a big part of these people's lives that I knew she would take the bait.

She did.

"I've seen you drink, Barbara," she sneered. "You're like a high school nerd trying to act like a cheerleader."

I wasn't quite sure what that meant, but if it meant she would take the challenge, that was good enough for me.

So we sat in my cabin at the little table, nose to nose, glaring at one another as we traded insults and ordered another round. Phil looked intimidated. We made him stand watch as a judge to make sure we drank our drinks. He couldn't believe two little old ladies could be so foulmouthed. I was learning all the things Lauren and her circle of friends had been saying behind my back to Octavian but he had been too polite to repeat.

And I was giving it my all too.

Oh yes, I can swear when I want to. I don't do it often, but three decades in the service has given me a repertoire that would make your average long-shoreman blush and send up several Hail Marys.

But not Lauren. She wasn't phased at all.

"Shall we make this more interesting?" Lauren snapped. "Shall we add some tequila to the mix?"

"Sure, assuming you don't hate Mexicans as much as you hate gay people."

"You're so ugly I'm surprised you haven't turned Octavian gay."

"I'm more of a woman than you'll ever be. If Octavian were gay, I'd straighten him out."

Oh my, did I say that? Phil looked ready to have a coronary. I should have checked the location of the nearest defibrillator.

Lauren snapped her fingers. Or at least tried to. Somehow her fingers missed each other, and she ended up waggling them in the air.

"Bill, er, Phil. Whatever your name is, bring us another round of piña coladas and a shot of tequila each."

"Right away, ma'am."

Phil looked glad to leave.

Lauren leaned close to me, wafting her boozy breath in my face. Her glassy eyes glittered with hatred.

"Octavian deserves someone better than you.

You're just a boring old fart. You've never done anything real in your whole life! I bet you've lived in Deerville or whatever it's called your whole life. Probably never been out of the country before now. You're just a boring old fart. That's what you are."

I laughed in her face. "I know why Georgina didn't send you to get Wesley away from Maggie. He would have never gone for you. Maggie had more class."

A crushed potato chip had more class than Lauren.

She didn't look surprised to hear those two names pass my lips.

"Oh, Octavian told you about our chat, did he? I bet he didn't mention what we were doing while we were chatting."

"Dancing around the cabin, I'm sure. Him running and you chasing."

Phil came back with the drinks. He was remarkably quick. I think he was as fascinated by this spectacle as he was repelled.

He set down our piña coladas and two shot glasses of tequila. Phil had picked gold tequila, and as I put my shot down, I realized he had given me apple juice. Good man.

I made a fake little shiver as if the alcohol was getting to me. Lauren gave me a look like a wolf gives when he sees a deer running slower than the rest of the herd.

"Hey, Bill, bring us some more," Lauren slurred. Despite her extensive experience in boozing, I could see she was beginning to flag.

"His name is Phil."

"Who cares? He's the help." She paused and looked uncertain for a moment, as if realizing she had been rude. "Oh, Bill, here's something for your trouble."

She pulled a five-dollar bill out of her purse and stuffed it down his trousers. I guess that was her idea of an apology. Phil looked like he was going to have a mental breakdown.

"Bring us the bottle," she ordered. "We have some real drinking to do."

Uh-oh.

Phil glanced at me. I didn't see a way out of it. I nodded.

Once he was gone, she glared at me again. I cut her off before she could start leaking toxic waste from her mouth.

"So why do you people go around poaching people's boyfriends and husbands?"

"Only boyfriends," she slurred. "You can't prove anything about the husbands."

"But why?"

She gave me a lopsided smile. "Because it's fun."

The tone didn't match her attitude. It came out hesitant, uncertain, as if she were trying to convince herself. A long silence settled over the table. She twirled her empty glass, staring at it. I let the silence extend. I was getting close. The alcohol had worked its magic, and her facade was crumbling.

Phil entered the room. "Sorry for being late, ladies. I got stopped in the hall."

"That's all right, Jill—I mean Bill—hee hee. Set 'em up." Lauren had rallied now that she had an audience again.

On his tray, Phil had a bottle of tequila. He gave me an apologetic look as he poured us each a shot and placed the bottle on the table.

"That will be all, Phil," I told him.

"Aw, come on!" Lauren bawled, sending spit across the table. "He should stay and watch us. He'll learn something about how real drinkers drink."

"That he would, but he's on duty, and he has other customers to serve."

She gave me a nasty smirk. "Like Octavian and whoever he's with."

Phil made his exit. Lauren raised her glass.

"Back to it," she ordered.

"Back to it," I said, trying to muster my courage.

The tequila went down like acid. I've never been much for straight shots, and this one was powerful.

Lauren immediately picked up the bottle, fumbled and nearly dropped it, and poured us another round.

"Down the hatch," she said.

Down the hatch they went.

And almost up the hatch again. My stomach, already aching from too much liquor the previous two days, rebelled. It took a conscious act of will to keep the tequila down.

Lauren bared her teeth. "Beginning to feel it, eh? What an amateur. Let's do another."

This time she did fumble the bottle, spilling tequila all over the table and on my dress. I grabbed the bottle before all of the contents were lost and poured the round myself. After stumbling to the bathroom and using a towel to mop up the mess, I fell back into my seat and picked up my drink. She did the same.

I looked her in the eye. Hers were glassy and unfocused. We took the third shot.

This time I was prepared for it and kept it down.

I couldn't stop the sick, wavering feeling that all but overcame me.

Lauren almost dropped her shot glass.

"I don't get you people," I said. "Stealing other people's men is bad enough, but making false allegations against Wesley just because Georgina couldn't get in some stupid book? That's low. And it hurts other women who have real allegations."

I did not expect the reaction I got.

Lauren burst into tears. The shot glass fell from her grasp and shattered on the table. She put her face in her hands and sobbed.

"It's terrible. Terrible! I can't take this anymore! Everyone is just so nasty, and you have to play along, otherwise you'll be next. And now Fiona and Brenda are sniping at one another about who made up the name for the team. Who cares? We're supposed to be friends. We're supposed to support each other. And now Alicia has had a heart attack. Will she ever recover? And to think that just the day before Georgina played a prank on her. Why, she could have had her heart attack there and then!"

"A prank? What sort of prank?"

"Oh, it was so juvenile. Alicia is afraid of spiders. Georgina bought a packet of those little plastic spiders and was going to ..." Lauren took in a long breath, her face turning a sickly color.

"Are you all right?" I asked.

"Urrggg ... BELCH. Oh!" She staggered to my bathroom and let loose. Most of it did not make it into the toilet.

After another minute of retching, she stumbled out of the bathroom. I had opened the porthole. It didn't help much. The stench was so bad I could have brought her up in front of a UN tribunal for using chemical weapons.

"Sorry," she mumbled, covering her mouth. She fumbled with the door, got it opened, and nearly fell into the hallway.

"What was Georgina going to do?" I asked.

"Huh? Urg, oh, I think I'm going to be sick again."

She stumbled across the hall and pounded on a cabin door. Fiona opened it, took one look at her, and slammed the door in her face. She ended up puking in the hallway.

Some roommate.

I rang for Phil, pulling out another hundred-dollar bill as a tip. The poor boy had earned it.

THIRTEEN

My next move was obvious, but getting it done was going to be tricky.

I needed to get a key card for Georgina's room, and I needed to get it right now.

In other words, I had to breach cruise ship security while drunk.

No sweat, right?

At least I knew what cabin she was in by process of elimination. Fiona opening the door for Lauren had left only one unidentified cabin on B Deck, Hall 5. That must be Georgina's cabin. She had her own, of course. No doubt so she could bathe in blood and hang from the ceiling like a bat without anyone bothering her.

The first thing I needed to do was get an employee ID card in order to access the computer system. That was easy enough. I just waited until Phil showed up and slipped it off the keychain dangling from his belt while he was having a panic attack about the vomit in my cabin and the unconscious senior citizen in the hallway.

"I'll call the cleaning service."

I left another hundred dollars in my cabin as a tip for the cleaning service. I filched the money from Lauren's purse.

No, that is not stealing. That is justice.

Next I needed a distraction, so it looked like poor Octavian had some more work to do. I knocked on his cabin door as Phil and the cleaning lady got Lauren to her feet and carried her off to the infirmary.

Octavian didn't answer. I knocked harder. Still no answer.

Uh-oh.

I called him. When he picked up, I asked, "Where are you?" I couldn't keep a slightly accusatory tone out of my voice. It was the tequila talking.

"In my cabin."

"I was just knocking on your door."

"You think I'm going to answer a knock with these hyenas prowling the hallway?"

He opened up then waved his hand in front of his face.

"Whew! You stink of tequila." He sniffed again. "What is that infernal miasma wafting from your cabin?"

I had left the door open. If I had to suffer, the entirety of B Deck, Hall 5 would have to suffer too.

"I had a drinking contest with Lauren. She lost. Now we need to steal a key card and sneak into Georgina's room."

"Right into the spider's web, eh? Count me in. What do I have to do?"

I told him my plan. My drunken plan. He looked dubious. I tried to calm his nerves. This was sure to work. I had thirty years in the CIA and a high blood alcohol content on my side, after all.

So ten minutes later we were at the concierge desk. Or more accurately, Octavian was at the concierge desk, and I was standing down the hall, pretending to look out a porthole.

Octavian strode up to the desk, slammed his hand down on it, and said "I demand a refund! This cruise is the worst I've ever taken in all my seventy-two years."

The young man behind the counter looked unphased. Night shift at a concierge desk on a cruise ship had no doubt given him ample experience in dealing with rude customers.

"First we get delayed because some poor woman is so frustrated by the bad service that she throws herself off the ship, then we get delayed again while you pick up the passengers from another ship, and now there's a big party going on in my hallway."

"What cabin is the noise coming from, sir? I can call and ask them to keep it down."

"Are you deaf? At your young age? It must be all that darned rock music you kids listen to. I said there was a party in my hallway. HALL. WAY. They're boozing it up in the hall, right outside my door. I nearly slipped on a pool of vomit just trying to get here!"

"I'm terribly sorry about that, sir. I'll send security."

"Security? No, I want you to come."

"But, sir, I need to stay at my—"

Octavian slammed his hand on the counter again. "You need to solve this problem immediately!"

I put my hand to my mouth to hide my smile. He was playing his role of the disagreeable old man admirably. The two young men walking by hand in hand agreed, judging by the scandalized looks they gave him.

The concierge went with him just to shut him up. Octavian led him in the opposite direction of his actual cabin. Hopefully he'd take him as far away as possible.

As soon as they were out of sight, Octavian's grumblings fading in the distance, I moved over to the concierge desk ...

... and moved away again. Some seniors were passing by.

As soon as they were gone, I went back to the desk, only to have to move away again because a waiter passed.

The third time I went, a young man came down the hallway. I stood in front of the counter like I was waiting for the concierge. He stood behind me for a moment as I fidgeted, looking around.

"Have you seen the concierge?" he asked.

"No, but I saw Tony Iron walk down the hallway a couple of minutes ago," I said, pointing.

His face lit up. "Really?" He ran off.

I got behind the counter and swiped Phil's card, and the computer gave me access. It only took a minute to find the key cards in the counter drawer and authorize one to open Georgina's cabin.

I logged off and got out from behind the counter just in time to avoid being spotted by another waiter.

Cruise ships sure are busy at night. Makes it hard to sneak about.

Now for phase two.

I went back to my hallway and saw the cleaning lady working on my room. It still stank. Wrinkling my nose, I knocked on the door of Octavian's cabin and found him already there.

"What did you do with the concierge?" I asked.

"Gave him the slip when he had to stop some young men from singing ABBA songs too loudly in the hallway."

"Good man. Now I need you to see if Georgina is in her cabin. If she is, ask her to go on a walk. Act interested. Keep her away for as long as you can."

"Doing that and remaining loyal to you might prove tricky."

"I know. I trust you. It's almost over. I hope."

I stayed in Octavian's room while he went over to Georgina's. I pressed a glass against the door and my ear against the glass.

Because the door was soundproofed to provide a sound sleep ("That's *Silver Siren* service for you!") I couldn't hear any words, only voices. Octavian was talking then Georgina. Then I heard a door shut, followed by silence.

I counted to ten and peeked out the door. The coast was clear. While the door to my cabin stood open, the cleaning lady was inside and could not see me. Considering the mess Lauren had left, she would be in there for some time.

The key card worked, and I slipped inside Georgina's cabin, quickly turning on the light and closing the door behind me.

That made me notice an interesting detail that I hadn't thought about before. In most hotels, the key card was also used to turn on the lights by sticking it in a slot just inside the door. Here they had a regular light switch. Someone could take your key card while you were in your cabin, and as long as you didn't leave and try to come back, you'd be none the wiser.

The cabin was identical to my own except with far more clothing and empty bottles. I started searching systematically through the drawers, closet, and bathroom then went through her luggage.

I didn't find what I was looking for until I searched the wastepaper basket.

A packet of plastic spiders. Unopened.

Georgina had not played that trick on Alicia, but Lauren had thought she had.

And why had she thought that?

Because Georgina said she was going to as a cover for stealing her key card.

Lauren probably caught her at it, and Georgina had to come up with an excuse. Being the wily woman she was, Georgina already had a cover story and a prop in place just in case that happened.

Georgina had switched more than the key card. She had switched the bowling ball. All the bowling-ball bags were identical, the same color with the same team logo. Only the individual color and name on each ball showed whose ball it was. Georgina had switched her ball with Alicia's well beforehand, an easy enough thing to do at any time, perhaps even before boarding ship, and Alicia wouldn't have known the difference until they had gone bowling. Before that happened, Georgina switched the key cards, committed the murder with Alicia's ball, and then exchanged balls once again, thus implicating Alicia.

The gang must have been drinking somewhere. Georgina would have had only a few minutes to commit the murder and switch the balls. She would have needed precise timing. But she knew when

Maggie would be standing at the prow. She must have gone to the dimly lit observation deck, saw Maggie standing there, and waited for the group to pass by so she could strike. With the wind and the waves, Maggie would not have heard her approach.

I had what I came for, now I needed to get out of here.

I listened to the door and heard nothing. I stepped out ...

... and nearly bumped into Lauren.

"What the heck are you doing in Georgina's cabin?" she demanded. She looked pale and haggard, but at least she was vertical. She had recovered from her binge drinking remarkably well. The power of experience.

"Wait. I can explain."

Lauren pulled her phone out of her pocket and speed-dialed a number. I stepped toward her, and she put out her hand, stepping back as she did so.

"You come any closer, and I'll scream," she said.

I heard a faint voice on her phone.

"Georgina? Guess what. I just caught Barbara breaking into your cabin."

I heard a curse on the other end of the line, and Georgina hung up.

Lauren sneered at me. "And now I'm going to call security and have you arrested."

"Lauren, wait. This is important. Georgina killed Maggie!"

"What? You're crazy. Maggie killed herself. She was always a loser."

"No. Listen. You saw Georgina steal Alicia's key card and replace it with her own, didn't you?"

Lauren gaped. "How could you know that?"

"Because that's how Georgina was going to get into Alicia's room to play the plastic-spider prank, except that's not why she really went in there. Alicia said she found her bowling ball covered in blood. Georgina used it to murder Maggie and left it in her room to incriminate her. She wasn't strong enough to push Maggie over the edge, and she wanted a fitting weapon to knock her off."

"But this is ridiculous. She—"

Lauren stopped as I opened the door, pulled out the unopened bag of plastic spiders, and held it up.

She gaped. For a second I thought she was going to throw up again. When she spoke next, her words came out in a ragged whisper. "She left the table the night Maggie died. She took Alicia's key card and left the table …"

"Where is she now? She took Octavian somewhere. Where did she go?"

Lauren leaned heavily against the wall. "We all talked about it. We all talked about killing her. I never thought one of us would actually go through with it ..."

I gripped her by the shoulders. "Where are they?"

"They went on deck. Georgina said she knew a nice dark place. I don't know where exactly."

My heart turned to ice. A nice dark place. Octavian thought he was playing his part, flirting with Georgina to cover me, but Georgina now had him in the perfect place to catch him unawares and push him over the edge.

Because she had heard I was onto her and knew that Octavian must be in on it too.

I started to run, knowing I may already be too late. Behind me, a door slammed.

FOURTEEN

I got on deck and breathed a sigh of relief. There were plenty of people around, but that didn't mean that Georgina wouldn't have a chance to make her move.

A dark place on deck. What place would be darker than the others? It all looked equally dim, the lights few and low so that people could admire the stars and have little trysts.

Perhaps I had guessed wrong, and they were on one of the upper decks? There were actually three decks, the main one and two higher ones on the ship's superstructure. But no, you couldn't push a man off the upper ones, because they were set in from the main deck. Even if she had gone up there with him, she would have led him down to the main one after being warned.

A shout from aft made me hurry in that direction.

I cursed my old legs, sore from last night's dance and wobbly from the aftereffects of three shots of tequila. I wasn't running. I was barely managing a fast walk.

There was another shout, a male cry.

"Octavian!"

I came around the corner and saw two figures struggling by the railing.

"Octavian!"

I blinked in the dim light as I drew closer. It was two young men tickling each other.

"Who's Octavian?" one asked.

I hurried on.

And then I saw two figures right at the tail end of the ship. One moved toward the other who quickly drew away. The first one followed, backing the other against a corner of the railing. No one else was in sight.

"Octavian!"

"Right here, pretty lady."

I moved over to the two shady figures, my legs

aching. Georgina had him cornered. Octavian was trying to keep her off as politely as he could.

"Get off him!" I demanded.

I could just barely make out Georgina's smug smile in the dim light.

"Why should I? He came to me. Looks like your little Octavian doesn't like you as much as you thought."

"It was a ruse," Octavian told her. "To get you out of the way."

"What?"

"I searched your cabin," I said, putting a restraining hand on her wrist, and Octavian squeezed out from the corner she had boxed him in. "I found that bag of plastic spiders. You never had any intention of putting them in Alicia's room. That was only a lie you told Lauren to cover up your real intentions: switching the bowling balls!"

Georgina looked confused. "What? Lauren gave me those spiders saying I should play the trick on Alicia. I said no and threw them in the trash. I never entered Alicia's cabin until we went in together."

"That sounds like a load of horse pucky," Octavian growled.

"You're a clever one, Georgina. I'll give you that.

You've been playing us all along, but I've found you out. I'm going to—"

I didn't get to finish my sentence. All of a sudden, Octavian pushed me to the side. I stumbled and fell, jarring my elbow.

Not that I'm complaining, mind you, because he saved me from the bowling ball that was coming right for my head.

Swung by Lauren.

She had crept up behind me and tried to brain me with her ball. Octavian had seen her at the last moment and pushed me aside.

But now Octavian had his own problems to contend with. Fiona was there, too, fingers gripped in the holes of her own bowling ball, which she swung like some medieval mace right for Octavian's face.

That kind, handsome face.

He ducked remarkably quickly considering his age. All that seniors' yoga had paid off, and instead of hitting Octavian, Fiona hit Georgina.

She grunted and slammed against the railing, her body bending and falling through the space between the bars. She dropped out of sight.

"No!" Fiona cried. She rounded on Octavian. "This is all your fault!"

While I struggled to rise, pain lancing through

my elbow, Fiona and Lauren closed in on him, backing him into the same corner that Georgina had.

"Oh, this is a problem," he muttered.

"It's all right to hit a lady in this situation!" I said.

"Really?" he asked, ducking another bowling ball.

"Really!"

He dodged an attack by Lauren then belted Fiona with an impressive right hook just as she was readying for another strike.

She toppled backward.

"Oh, I am so sorry!" Octavian shouted, getting on his knees and grabbing her hand. "Are you all right?"

He was so flustered by acting ungentlemanly that he didn't notice Lauren right over him, raising her bowling ball for the kill. I got to my feet but then fell again, my legs buckling because of the strain, the tequila, and just darned old age. My eyes widened as the bowling ball swung down straight at the skull of the man I loved ...

... to be stopped by a pair of strong hands.

"Ow!" the newcomer shouted. I blinked.

It was Tony Iron.

Using his famous muscles, he wrenched the ball from Lauren, who hissed in pain as her fingers got scraped from the holes in the ball.

"What's going on here?" the music legend demanded.

Three young men moved in and got between all the combatants.

I pointed at Fiona and Lauren. "These two killed Margaret Underwood!"

"No, we didn't. You killed Georgina!" Lauren shouted.

Then we were all shouting at once, hurling accusations and counteraccusations.

Tony Iron looked at each of us, not sure who to believe.

"Heeelp!" Georgina's voice came from below.

We all looked over the railing.

Several feet below us, and still high above the churning water of the propeller, Georgina hung tangled on the flagpole. She had fallen in just the right way that the flagpole had caught her dress, the flag itself tangling with her to help stop her fall.

It was a million-to-one stroke of luck, and it had to happen to someone like her.

"Heeelp!" she cried again. I heard a tearing sound, and her body lurched downward, stopping after a few inches.

"Her dress is tearing," I said. "We have to get her now."

"I'll call security!" one of the young men said, rushing to find the nearest courtesy phone. I knew help wouldn't come in time.

"We have to save her!" Fiona cried.

I spotted a ring-shaped life preserver hanging from the railing nearby. I hobbled over and grabbed it. It had a long line of thin but strong rope. The other end was affixed to the steel railing. I got right above Georgina, who was flailing in panic and only succeeding in tearing her dress more, and lowered it down. With my aching elbow, I didn't dare try to throw it.

"Get it around you and hang on!" I called.

"Take care, Georgina!" Lauren shouted. She and Fiona were right at the edge of the railing, looking panicked. A minute before, they had been trying to kill us, and now all they cared about was their leader.

The life preserver got down to her, and she stuck it around her middle. The two remaining young men and Tony Iron hauled on the rope. She didn't budge. They pulled again, and there was a tearing sound as her dress fell away.

"Oh my," Octavian said, averting his eyes. He didn't need to, because that wasn't the only thing that tore.

The flag tore, too, and as she was hauled up, she

wrapped Old Glory around herself to hide her old ... glory.

"Now that's what I call a patriot," Tony Iron said as he helped her over the railing.

Georgina gave him a grin. "That's me: red, white, and true blue." She pointed at Lauren and Fiona. "Call security, and have those two arrested. They killed Margaret Underwood and tried to frame me for it!"

Lauren burst into tears, real ones this time. I think. She was really good at faking emotions. She had played me like a fiddle, and I had gone after the wrong woman, almost getting myself and Octavian killed in the process.

Oh, and Georgina, I guess I should count her.

"We did it for you, Georgina," Lauren bawled. "We did it all for you!"

Fiona nodded. "Maggie was destroying everything. You know how the judge let Wesley off? That was because of her."

"No, that was because of your lousy reputation," I cut in.

The three "ladies" ignored me.

Georgina sobbed. "I never wanted you to kill her. Now look what you've done! How can we win the next tournament if two of the Six Mouseyketeers are in jail?"

In. Credible.

"We're sorry. We are so sorry," Fiona said, adding her tears to Lauren's.

"But why did you implicate Alicia?" Georgina demanded. "She was your friend!"

"She was beginning to take Brenda's side," Fiona said. "Stealing the idea of the team name from me! I switched our bowling balls as the stevedore took our luggage while we waited in line. I'd been going into her cabin to check her vitals. Last night, when I realized she wasn't going to tell anyone about her bowling ball having blood on it, I decided to get rid of the evidence. I told her to have a long, hot shower before taking a nap. That's when I got rid of the ball. I just took it on deck, waited until no one was looking, and chucked it overboard."

"We did it all for you, Georgina," Lauren insisted. "And when these two old bats started sniffing around, we had to divert them to protect you."

"That's simply not true," Octavian said. "You spun that tale about the plastic spiders to get us off the scent, to make us think Georgina was the murderer. You may have started by doing it for your little group, but when we got too close, you sold out the woman you so admire."

Lauren's mouth worked, unable to come up with a reply. Just then the ship's security showed up, three burly sailors who looked confused as to just who to arrest.

Fiona cleared them up on that account by collapsing at their feet. "We did it for Georgina!" she shrieked. "We did it for Georgina!"

Georgina leveled her finger at Fiona then at Lauren, like a witch pronouncing a curse. Considering what she said next, she might as well have been. "Lauren, Fiona, you are no longer my friends."

Security took the two wailing women away.

Georgina put an arm around Tony Iron and gave him a sultry smile. "When you fish a mermaid out of the sea, isn't it traditional to give her a kiss?"

"Lady, I have had some of the sexiest, most alluring women in the world throw themselves at me." Tony Iron detached himself none too gently. "And you are not one of them."

He put his arms around his young male companions and sauntered off.

FIFTEEN

Late the next morning, after a very long night explaining everything to the ship's security and seeing the two murderers confined to the ship's small jail cell, Octavian and I walked along the deck. We found ourselves drifting to the prow, where Maggie had paid tribute to the one happy period of her life and got killed for it.

"So petty," Octavian muttered.

"Most murders are petty when you really look at them. People rarely kill each other for any good reason. They usually kill because they're selfish and the victim threatens their selfish desires."

Octavian shook his head, looking out across the glittering Caribbean. "What an ugly world you had to live in, Barbara."

"Yes, working at the CIA could get ugly at times, but we were trying to make the world less ugly." I cozied up to him. "And my life is looking a lot more handsome these days."

He sighed. "It's too bad we couldn't save Maggie."

"We didn't know she was in danger until she was already dead. And we saved Georgina's life, not to mention our own."

He looked at me. "I want you to know that I have never hit a lady before in all my life."

I put my hand on his. "You still haven't hit a lady."

Octavian nodded and looked back out to sea, not speaking for a moment. Then he turned and kissed me. "Promise me one thing," he said.

"Anything. I think you've earned it," I replied, kissing him again.

"Promise me the next time we go on vacation that no one will get murdered."

I smiled, relieved. I was beginning to wonder if there would be a next vacation, considering how this one turned out.

"Unfortunately I can't promise that. How about I pay for the next vacation? You have a birthday coming up, I suppose."

"They come faster and faster with each passing year."

"Hmmm, they do indeed. All right, it's settled. I'll pay for the vacation."

"It's not about who pays. It's about the bloody murders and hunting after suspects," Octavian grumbled.

"I suppose it's not everyone's idea of a romantic getaway."

"No, it is not. The strange thing is it's really piqued my appetite. Why don't we go to our cabins, freshen up, and head on over to that twenty-four-hour buffet?"

"All right."

A few minutes later, coming out of my cabin, I saw Octavian already in the hallway. Georgina was just entering her cabin, casting a smile over her shoulder at him.

I went up to him after her door closed. "Don't tell me she was flirting with you after all this."

He looked aggrieved. "Even worse. She asked me for my Facebook."

"You poor thing! What did you do?"

Octavian hung his head. "I said I didn't have an account."

"But you do?"

He nodded. "Yeah. My kids made me get it."

"I've been spared. My son thinks it's stupid, my daughter is too busy, and my grandson says it's for old people. I only got an account yesterday to check on Maggie's status updates. Do you actually feel guilty about lying to Georgina?"

Octavian smiled, looking quite content. "No, it was just a passing phase, like punching a bowling-ball-wielding murderer intent on killing me. I have an idea. Let's stuff ourselves at that buffet, and tonight let's go hear the world's greatest has-beens and dance like a pair of old fools pretending they're sixteen. And tomorrow we finally dock at a beautiful Caribbean island. I say we go on shore, drink some tropical fruit juice—no more alcohol, for God's sake have mercy—and then we walk hand in hand on a pristine beach while the locals try to sell us shell necklaces and straw hats at inflated prices."

"Sounds good to me," I replied, taking him by the arm as we walked down the hallway.

I was wrong. It wasn't just good. It was wonderful.

ABOUT THE AUTHOR

Harper Lin is a *USA TODAY* bestselling cozy mystery author. When she's not reading or writing mysteries, she loves going to yoga classes, hiking, and hanging out with her family and friends.

For a complete list of her books by series, visit her website.

www.HarperLin.com

www.ingramcontent.com/pod-product-compliance
Lightning Source LLC
Chambersburg PA
CBHW050853180626
46814CB00007B/2747